THE FOUNDATION

A Timeless Adirondack Adventure

By

Captain Samuel Dean

THE FOUNDATION

A Timeless Adirondack Adventure

Copyright © 2019

Samuel Dean

Godspeed Loj Publishing

Dedication:

This story is dedicated with loving memory to Dr. Robert Dorrance Ph.D.—Professor Emeritus, natural historian, lover of the Adirondacks, and a mentor to all who knew him.

"We don't own Adirondack land; we merely own the responsibility to it."

DR. ROBERT DORRANCE

CONTENTS

THE SPIRIT OF
THE STONE

T hey explored the whole rest of our country before they even named this place. And after the settling of America, they called it a lot of things, like "The Dismal Wilderness," or "Deer Hunting Country," and my favorite, "Habitation of Winter," a name that recently changed to "The Siberia of America." In fact, it wasn't until Samuel de Champlain's Iroquois guide misinterpreted his inquiry did this country get its final name. According to the legend, Champlain was canoeing on the lake that now bears his name, and upon seeing the High Peaks, Champlain asked his guide, "What are those mountains called?" The guide misinterpreted the question as "who lives in those mountains?" and answered "Ha-De-Ron-Dah" or "those who eat trees." This was a dig at the competition, the Algonquin tribe, who used these woods as their hunting ground when the Iroquois weren't hunting them. A lot of modern sages now believe the Indian guide was describing the ubiquitous beaver that also inhabited the area, but I think they're just trying to be politically correct because no self-respecting Iroquois would pass up an opportunity to insult an Algonquin, for the tribes hated each other.

Over time, via the various dialects of the white men who tried to tame this land, "Ha-De-Ron-Dah" was pronounced "Adirondack," and thus the Park was born. Despite the state campgrounds, family picnics, the Enchanted Forest, and even the Lake Placid Brew Pub, this land is still untamed. I wasn't kidding when I said the rest of the United States had been explored and settled long before the Adirondacks were. In fact, the headwaters of the Colorado River were known for a full sixty years before Lake Tear of the Clouds, the source of the Hudson, was discovered. Even the Algonquin and Iroquois, who tramped this land, never settled here. There are also forty-six High Peak mountains in the northeast quad that the natives never wasted their time by climbing. Archeologists claim this to be true because they have found none of their artifacts atop any of these peaks. But it's a misnomer to call them "high" peaks, especially since the city of Denver is about half of a mile higher than the highest Adirondack mountain. They are really more like steep hills, but at least the trees grow all the way to the top of most of their summits. I've climbed a bunch of them when I was younger but documented none, so I'll need to start over when I want to earn my 46er patch. That's a goal I've put off until my seventies, which is something you can't do if you're planning on climbing the Alps. Besides, the summit trails are so busy these days. And while I'll gladly give way to a mother pushing a baby carriage (something I had to do once on the crowded trail to Mt. Marcy), it is vexing when I almost get run over by the Olympic wannabes, who sprint up the mountain trails while wearing nothing but spandex and sports bras. I know better than to dress like this because one of the worst snowstorms I've ever been in was when I summited Algonquin Peak, and that was in June! A lot of people don't pack properly or even carry a pack when they climb these hills; and because of their foolishness, they come down only when the forest rangers carry them down, either on a Stokes litter or in a body bag. The rangers have a term for this—they call it "overtime."

So I avoid the congestion of the trails by hiking and hunting in the state-designated Wilderness Areas. These are huge, isolated tracts of wild forest where a man can visit but not stay. In these primitive areas, there are no motor vehicles, no structures, and no trails. It's a primal paradise, untouched by time; a tangled wilderness, full of mystery, and for some—magic.

The Algonquin had a name for these magical places: *Manitou-Hassun*, which white men have translated as "Spirit Stone". I think it is a mistake to believe the Algonquin were referring to a particular stone or rock, especially since the Adirondacks are filled with them. I can recall feeling pretty stupid when I asked a local landscaper where I could buy stone for a fireplace I was building.

He said, "Just stick your shovel in the ground and try to dig. You'll find all the stone you need—for free!"

Damn, if he wasn't right. During the last known Ice Age, the glaciers deposited all of Canada's rocks right here. I find them whenever I try to mow the few sprigs of grass that grow on my little patch of lawn. I often think what a cruel trick it was for our impoverished country to pay our Civil War soldiers by giving them Adirondack land to farm. The poor, rocky soils and short growing season of this region practically ensured their agricultural failure. This is why I think the Algonquin meant that Manitou-Hassun relates to a spiritual *place*, rather than a mere stone.

Not long ago, when I was tramping in the McKenzie Wilderness, I found one of these Spirit Places. I should have left it alone, but like a moth to a flame, it drew me to it, and I kept returning. But unlike the moth, the flame of the Spirit Place didn't consume me—instead, it gave me some incredible experiences, and some of them were downright dangerous. But through those adventures, I experienced another life—maybe even more than one.

This is the story of one of those lives. I'm just not sure of which one.

CHAPTER 1

My name is Mason Brocke, and I consider myself an Adirondack native because I was born here, but I've been away for most of my life. Eighteen years ago, I moved back to the North Country, only by then, they called it a "Park." The common term up here for "a native" is "a local"—as in *"Oh, yah, you is a local boy, no?"* I would immediately destroy my local status if I ever openly referred to where I live as *a park.* The real locals hate that almost as much as they hate the Adirondack Park Agency, Democratic politicians, and The New York State SAFE Act. Likewise, the only reference that a local should make to The Blue Line (the line that delineates the Adirondack Park on maps) is to either be talking about the brewery or gin of that name. In the past eighteen years, I've even picked up the half-assed Canadian accent fairly well. I usually say *"yah"* for yes, *"thot"* for that, *"wot"* for want (or what), and *"mut beer"* for up here. Also, when someone asks where I am, I say, *"I'm over to* Lake Clear," which is better English than the typical "I'm over at" response. Sometimes it still takes me a minute or two to translate a particular string of words (called a *senence* up here). For example, *"Der ain't many adem peckerwoods mut beer"* means "there aren't many of those hardwood trees up here." *Yah,* I'm happy to be a local.

My wife Marlene will never be considered a local. While she's lived up here (*mut beer, for you locals*) as long as I have, she has never lost her shit-eating Long Island accent. In fact, I think sometimes she exaggerates it, especially when she's showing her clients' one of those quintessential cottages on a lake. I'm sure she does this intentionally to communicate more effect-ively with her prospects, as they often list these lakefront real estate prices in shorthand as $1.5M—meaning a million and a half bucks. Most of her exclusive clientele are from Long Island, New Jersey, or Canada. I guess that the wealthy Canadians don't mind her accent as much as I do and probably think it's the way everyone speaks down here (the inverse of *mut beer*). But des-pite the accent, her urbane sophistication, and an aura of super-iority, I'm still madly in love with her—despite my feelings of inadequacy, jealousy, and inferiority. *Opposites attract, right?*

Even though the records show I'm only fifty-four, I got retired from the state in 2008. I say "got retired" because I really didn't have much of a choice. I was working in Ray Brook as a wildlife biologist when the poop hit the propeller. This was my dream job and what my bachelor's degree is in. But when the great re-cession hit, Wall Street stopped paying their million-dollar bo-nuses, and my employer, the State of New York, went into finan-cial shock from the consequential tax starvation. The crisis soon trickled down to the multitude of state agencies and took its toll on their employees. As a result, New York State offered me a retirement incentive, which is just a kind way of laying you off with dignity. But I'm lucky because while I get little in the way of a pension, I have good medical insurance. In fact, my coverage is so good that somehow Marlene gets her Mirror Lake Inn Spa visits covered under my plan. Infrequently, she'll men-tion how nice this is, but more often *I think* she complains about my paltry pension. Occasionally, I'll catch a glimpse of one of her commission checks and know why. I see none of this money (did I mention that on the advice of Marlene's parental attor-ney, our bank accounts and finances are separate), and so to re-duce my inadequacy, I took the single option. When you take a state retirement, you get a once-in-a-lifetime chance to split your pension with your spouse, at a reduced benefit, or take the whole shot by selecting the single option. I did this because it made me feel independent, but Marlene won't get a dime when

I croak. Occasionally, I feel guilty, but not for long because I know she'll just ask her daddy for a raise in her monthly allowance to cover her healthcare. She'll also have to pay for her spa treatments too.

Marlene can spend money faster than a drunken sailor, and no one wants to hire a fifty-something-year-old biologist, especially up here. Hell, I had to move to Long Island for my first job, and I was in my twenties. But that's the way it is in the North Country; you either wait tables, clean cabins, and lacquer pinecones (to sell as souvenirs), or if you're lucky, you work for the state. Since my luck ran out, I do handyman contracting, which involves crazy things like roofing during the summer and shoveling snow off them during winter. I pretend this keeps Marlene's luxury SUV from being repossessed and pays for the satellite internet (Marlene said DSL wasn't fast enough for her real estate business) and our solar- and wind-augmented electric service (wouldn't want Marlene's rarely used hot-tub to freeze). Deep down, I know this is nonsense because Marlene can easily pay our bills and can take care of herself. But a man's got to feel important.

I do way more roof shoveling than roofing because winter lasts a while mut beer. Occasionally, I'll get to build a deck for someone's camp, but it's very competitive and rarely do I land a good-paying job. That's because the "cor-tractors" from Dannemora Prison can easily outbid me. These guys work their three-day-a-week jobs as corrections officers and have side businesses as contractors. Because of their no-show jobs, they're flush with cash and time. They also have the best tools and the biggest new trucks and trailers. And since these cor-tractors live near Plattsburgh, they can buy their materials dirt cheap from Lowes instead of that over-priced Durkis Lumber. They can even afford to hire local mutts like me to work their jobs. Occasionally, they've offered to sub me a job, but my foolish pride won't allow me to work for a prison guard. The other advantage that the cor-tractors have over me is that I've fallen into the Adirondack contractor's tradition of never passing up a good day of hunting or fishing instead of working. So it's decks, roofing, and shoveling for me. I tried plowing snow for a while, but my over-stressed '89 Dodge pickup wasn't up to it. I spent more time fixing it than plowing, so it's just my daily ride now. And to be honest, I love parking it next to Marlene's SUV. Someday, I'll get a new used truck.

I had a few camp caretaking contracts, but they dried up with the invention of smart home technology, although I still get a few calls when the heat is out or the roof sensors detect an excessive snow load. A few owners of these Great Camps have asked me to stay on as a cleaner after Memorial Day, but again my pride won't let me be a housemaid for these oversized lake-front mansions. Besides, playing janitor all summer would con-flict with the one part-time gig that I don't mind doing, which is teaching. I'm an adjunct professor at Paul Smith's College, but I only teach one course: Adirondack Biology 101.

A few decades ago, I took this class when I was attending Environmental Science and Forestry College back in 1974. It was two weeks of intensive fieldwork at the Cranberry Lake Bio-logical Field Station. Since it was all field work, a lean-to served as our lecture hall and we camped in the woods during the en-tire course. The curriculum was hands-on as well. We would do flushing counts during the day, and before nightfall, we'd set live traps in grids to do species-specific population estimates. I filled many a composition notebook with notes, which I con-tinue to use when I teach. It was a great course, but the greatest thing about it was our professor, Dr. Robert Torrance. His Ph.D. may have been in biology, but I think his passion was history, Adirondack history to be precise. Tall, lean, and athletic, the sixty-year-young professor could climb mountains with a pace that left his students breathless. But the reward for keeping up with him was priceless because he lectured while he hiked, and he greatly enriched those of us who were fit enough to stay within earshot of his melodious voice. Every night, when the work was done, we'd sit around the campfire and attentively listen to his stories and lessons about the Adirondacks. He covered everything from the geologic formations of the High Peaks to the bloody sea battles on Lake Champlain. While Dr. Torrance was an outstanding classroom lecturer, his fireside storytelling was absolutely enthralling. I was so riveted by his non-fiction tales I still remember them. I also know his fireside lessons are the reason I moved back to the Park and still appreciate this unspoiled land today.

So, to the best of my ability, I copied the course. But to be honest, I'm not qualified to be a college professor. I got the job because of my former position as a wildlife biologist. When I approached the college board with my idea, they thought it was a good one (read: tuition revenue producer), and approved my curriculum. Turns out they were right because the course is extremely popular and even has a waiting list most years. While I'd like to think the reason for this is my scintillating and captivating style of teaching, I know that it's also because AB101 awards three easy credit hours for just two weeks of camping fun. To add value to the course, I've copied my former mentor's style of having campfire Adirondack history lessons, but I'm no Dr. Torrance. As I'm telling a story, I know that the kids can't wait for me to shut up and turn in so they can smoke dope and spawn (this is perhaps another reason for the course's popularity). I feel like I should finish each session with a lecture on Effective Birth Control Methods and Date-Rape Drug Awareness, but their parents would probably sue me. Regardless, I still enjoy teaching this course and won't miss it by working the summer as a housemaid, even though that job would pay better.

CHAPTER 2

I remember the first time I saw the foundation.

It was after the January thaw and the snow was perfect for snowshoeing. With no other paying jobs, I thought I'd go looking for "sheds" in the woods. Sheds are antlers that the bucks drop during winter so they can better negotiate cedar swamps and spruce thickets. These swamps and thickets would be impenetrable for a twelve-point buck, but sans antlers they can crawl through them just fine. Of course, you don't see any twelve-pointers up here (notice I've stopped with the local language). The best I've ever found is a ten-point, but usually sixes and eights are the norm. The North Country climate is too harsh for a deer to waste food on growing big antlers. By the way, I make chandeliers and lamps with these antlers. They are popular with the tourists and "Great Campers" and fetch me a good buck. I like them, too, but Marlene would go *beaucoup'* ape-shit if I ever hung one of these in our house. So I sell them. I've even sacrificed the antlers on my trophy mounts (that hung in my garage) to make lamps. They were mule deer from when I did my internship out West. But, lucky for me, most of the tourists don't know the difference between native whitetails or western mules and they probably think the bifurcated tines are cool. After all, they only want a piece of (what they believe is) rustic Adirondack elegance to display at home. I'm jealous.

So I threw my snowshoes and my antler-carrying duffel bag in the truck, along with my butt pack, and headed to Moose Pond. Most of the road to the pond is closed this time of the year, but you can access the McKenzie Wilderness from anywhere along the east of the plowed portion. After parking and outfitting, I snowshoed south, toward the pond, until I observed a well-used deer path and followed it. The trail was wide, so I figured this must surely be a buck path. Hence my hopes were up for a productive day.

After about a half of an hour of prospecting, I hadn't found a thing except hoof prints. I also realized I'd been ascending the whole time and guestimated that my elevation was about two thousand feet. No wonder why I was getting tuckered out. I could have confirmed my elevation by firing up the GPS in my butt pack but didn't want to wait for it to sync under the thick canopy of pines. Most time you've got to find a clearing for those things to work in these dense forests. Besides, my pin-on compass told me all that I needed to know—specifically that I'd been walking southeasterly, toward the saddle between Moose and McKenzie mountains.

Onward I bushwhacked through a raised bed of a scraggly spruce-fir thicket. Tall white pines and tamaracks bordered each side of the thicket, almost like it had once been a trail. With this perception, I realized this was a human-made road! Long ago, some industrious soul had even piled stones to level the slope and make bridges over gullies. I tried to recall if the State had ever made a trail to the Moose or McKenzie summits, but decided this was unlikely because these weren't High Peaks or even desirable mountains to climb. Besides, by the understory growth, I could tell that this roadway predated any turn-of-the-last-century's public works projects. *Yet, someone had made it.* I trudged on.

After another half hour of shoeing, I observed the low winter sun was lower, and calculated I had about an hour of nautical twilight to follow my tracks out. I had a headlamp in my pack, but those damn things never shine bright enough to light up the branches that steal your hat and slap your face. As I was about to come about, I noticed a significant depression in the snow ahead. I had to check it out, but I should have just turned around.

What I saw was fantastic! It was a rock-lined, square crater, and it took me a moment to realize that I had found an olden house foundation—smack dab in the middle of the wilderness! I also realized the old roadway I followed was most likely made by the inhabitants of this structure. *But how long ago, and who had lived here?* The foundation formed a cellar constructed of huge, precisely fitted rocks piled upon each other. These un-cemented, moss-covered stone walls made a rectangular base of about twenty by twenty-four feet. Any evidence of an or-ganic structure (most likely a log cabin) was long gone; in its place were several mature birch trees growing up from what used to be the cellar floor. The walls were in good shape except for a pile of angular stones along one wall. I reasoned that this was the fireplace, the heart of the domicile, where cooking oc-curred and warmth emerged. I reasoned it had collapsed a long time ago by the thick sphagnum moss that grew on top of the stone pile. I estimated the cellar to be about six-feet deep, and several of the birch trees had died within its perimeter. They were about eighteen inches in diameter when their sap ceased to flow, and now black, horse-hoof mushrooms decorated their paper-white bark.

Forgetting it was getting late, I used the rock ramp of the fallen fireplace to climb down into the cellar. I found myself standing on a solid floor albeit filled with leaves about a foot deep. *But why wasn't it filled with snow?* As that thought passed, I noticed that it was much warmer in the cellar. It was like in-floor heat was emanating from the ground, which is why there wasn't snow on the floor. As I shuffled through the leaves, check-ing the mason's primitive craftsmanship, I became awestruck. *How could someone have accomplished this?* More than a few of the foundation rocks were boulders of over two feet in diam-eter. I knew from the experience of digging out rocks from my yard that these stones weighed over 800 pounds. And yet, here

Samuel Dean

they were, six feet below grade and set upon each other, forming perfectly plumb walls to make a foundation for some intrepid soul's home. More likely, it was a family's homestead because a cellar would be an unnecessary extravagance for a trapper's seasonal cabin. *But how did they do it, how did they live and get on through winter and who were they?* What a mystery!

I recalled from my *Adirondack Reader* that during the Revolutionary and Civil Wars our government couldn't afford to pay soldiers, so it gave them land to farm. What a cruel trick it was to give land in the Adirondacks to an unknowing soldier for farming. That's because combined with a short growing season, the soil of this region is "boney" (infused with rocks from glaciers), and it's poor in the nutrients needed for growing crops. To those unfamiliar with this terrain, looking at the lush, dense forests that grow up from it, one would never accuse this soil of being poor for growing crops. I recalled from my college days that geologists classify the Adirondack region as a temperate rainforest, and like their tropical counterpart, the nutrients are in the flora, not the soil. That means when you remove the trees, you take the nutrients with them. What's left is sandy, rocky, glacial till suitable for growing lichen and mosses but not corn or wheat. As many a Brazilian coffee farmer has discovered (after ruining a rainforest by clearing an area the size of Rhode Island) the added cost of fertilizer to grow crops makes the venture unprofitable. It's the same here.

I climbed out of the cellar and walked the perimeter of the foundation, which gave me a peculiar feeling of going back in time. The foundation was sited well, on a raised knoll with excellent views of the surrounding peaks. It even had a commanding view of Whiteface's summit; its jagged peak was brilliantly gleaming in the late afternoon sun. As I looked around, I had visions of the way the land must have appeared from the cabin's windows, with cleared fields and with animals grazing.

The lengthening shadows of the setting sun interrupted my reminiscences. It was time to get moving, and since I had no idea where I was, I broke out my tritium lensatic compass. As I set the azimuth back to Moose Pond Road, I noted that the direct route lie along the homestead's old access road. As such, I backtracked on the trail made by the herds of deer that now had its exclusive use, but I didn't find any sheds. As I followed my old tracks, I appreciated that without stumbling on this road I would never have found the foundation. It is amazing the things a man doesn't see unless he's looking for them! I kept following the road to an unfamiliar muskeg forest where the vector to the road was now at a right angle to my path. This was odd because my previous azimuth showed that it was in direct alignment with the old road. Also, I noted that my tracks had ended. *Was there an iron ore deposit that was creating a magnetic anomaly here, or did my compass just go wacky?* The shadows were gone now because the sun had set. I had to get serious about finding my way to the truck, so I trusted the compass (like you're supposed to when you're lost) and left the old road. After about twenty face-swatting minutes of bushwhacking in the dark, I reached the road and found my truck, right where I had left it.

That winter, I vowed to return to the foundation, but despite my best effort, I wasn't able to find the foundation or the old road. Sometimes, I wondered if I ever had. I should have marked it with my GPS, but for some primal reason, I don't think of using technology when I'm in the wilderness. I now wish that I had, because I couldn't stop thinking about that damn foundation, and nearly froze my ass off in my quest to find it again.

I shouldn't have tried to find it. Because I did, and as they say up here—*"it's weird how thot works."*

CHAPTER 3

When I got home, I found a note from Marlene stating that she had a Realtor's meeting in Lake Placid and would be home late. I used to think these incessant real estate agent meetings were just "girls' night out" events, but lately, I had to remind myself that a fair number of real estate agents have swinging dicks. I should pay better attention to this. Marlene's note also said, "There is a roast with potatoes and gravy warming in the oven, prepared just the way you like—bon appétit!" This, fortunately, was nonsense because Marlene couldn't cook, and would never even consider leaving a TV dinner for me. I know she loves me, just not in a homemaking way. What's the old saying? "Cooking lasts, kissing doesn't." *Maybe I've got that saying backwards?* To be honest, I was glad because it made me feel less guilty for stopping at the Downtowne Grille for dinner and having a pint, or maybe two. A man gets both hungry and thirsty in these woods.

Out of habit, I checked the phone for messages, which is a useless practice since no one ever called for me. But there was a call for Marlene, and a message from her Uncle Thaddaeus. He had built one of those palatial Great Camps on an island that he owned over to Rainbow Lake. Thaddaeus was actually a fairly down-to-earth guy for a Long Islander. Uncle "Ted" (and you never called him that) had always treated me with respect, and occasionally, I even got a few odd jobs from him. I always offered to give him the "family" discount (meaning free labor), but to my surprise, he always insisted on paying, and being from a foreign, wealthy country—like Long Island—he paid pretty damn well! This was probably another reason I liked him. I smelled money, so I thought I'd better listen to see what Uncle Ted was up to.

After listening for several minutes to what I thought was the best imitation of Elmer Fudd's voice ever, Uncle Ted finally got around to the purpose of his call: *"Marla, deah, if you wood be so kind as to have Mason cleah Camp Thady's woof, I wood appwreeshiate it gwreatly. My webcam shows dat da snow is getting wather deep and fweezing wain is forecast for lader dis week."*

That's the way it always was. No one in Marlene's family ever contacted me directly, even Uncle Ted, but at least he was a paying customer.

The following morning, I dug my crawdad out from under the snow pile by the woodshed and threw it, along with a paddle and a shovel, in the truck. I should have thrown in a life jacket, too, but I've got into the North Country habit of not wearing one because they're called "body finders" up here. Those of you who are not nautically inclined are probably wondering what type of vessel a "crawdad" is. It is a small, square-ended, flat-bottomed boat that mariners call a "pram." It is the perfect craft for pushing over thin ice while you're walking behind it. That way if the ice breaks, you can just jump in the boat with only a wet foot. I didn't yet trust Rainbow Lake's ice because there were too many islands, each creating ice-thinning counter-currents. In February, you can drive a truck across it, but this soon after the January thaw you'd better push your crawdad.

Thinking about the thin ice made me think about ice fishing on Franklin Flow. I figured that I'd finish with Uncle Ted's roof by early afternoon, which should give me plenty of time to catch some pike for dinner. To be honest, I would quit by noon, for although the weather service forecasted the temperature to stay in the teens, they also forecasted a bright, sunny day. I learned from experience, you don't want to be standing on a metal roof during a sunny afternoon, for the subsequent thawing and flash freezing makes them slipperier than a rotten banana peel. With that pleasant thought, I threw my ice-chopping spudger and fishing tip-ups in the truck and headed out.

Uncle Ted's camp was a picture-postcard beauty, built in the Adirondack Style during the eighties. Its construction was a combination of materials with exquisite flairs of cedar shakes, rough-cut timbers, and native granite stone with massive log trusses. It also had a metal roof, which is pretty much a standard feature on both big, expensive houses and little tarpaper shacks up here. Metal roofing is preferred because it sheds snow quicker than an indoor Siberian Husky sheds fur. So why, you may wonder, did this roof need to be shoveled? The answer is because this beautiful Adirondack Great Camp was designed by a Manhattan architectural firm, who had no idea what a North Country winter was like. Consequently, there isn't enough pitch on the roof for the snow to calve-off until it reaches a depth and weight of damaging proportions. I say damaging because these numbnut architects also included an aesthetic roofline of lower-story roofs under upper-story roof eves—allowing heavy snow and ice to crash down on the lower levels with tumultuous force. This ridiculous design even included several unsheltered decks for the avalanches to demolish, including their artsy-fartsy twig railings.

Poor Uncle Ted had been clueless about this design flaw until he got his first spring repair bill. Since then, he's called me to *cleah dah woof* whenever his expensive solar-powered webcam shows him *dat dah snow is getting wather deep*. I feel for him, but it's not like he can't afford the recurring costs of maintaining his summer camp (his winter camp is in Barbados). At least Uncle Ted is intrepid enough to own and sustain a place up here, unlike Marlene's parents, Reginald and Darlene (I call them Reggie and Darla to annoy them, but when I really want to piss them off, I call them Mom and Dad). They own a condo at the Whiteface Resort, which they call their "ski hut." In the past, Reggie and Darla would invite Marlene and me over for dinner at the resort's Canu restaurant whenever they came up for their annual ski holiday. They haven't extended this invite to me during the last several years—*I must have called them Mom and Dad too many times?*

The Canu is a great place to dine if you appreciate faux rustic decor and overpriced food and drink. Since I don't have the highly evolved palate, *or the personality,* that allows me to taste a tiny scrap of beef, fish, or fowl and lie about how good it is, dining at the Canu is a waste for me. I prefer pub-style, hardy fare and plenty of it—that's true Adirondack fine dining. As for the Canu's decor, I ask—how many fake logs, fake antler lamps, and artificial birch bark can you look at before you no longer see any of it? It's kind of over the top decor, like the Dartbrook store exploded and all the rustics landed at the resort. But, to be honest, I can't fault these artificial Adirondack places too much; at least they give less-fortunate people (like Wall Street billionaires) a flavor of this land and a chance to enjoy it. When I was a student attending conferences at the Lake Placid Crowne Pointe Hotel, those fake timbers and gas fireplaces intensified my desire to live up here (but not half as much as Dr. Torrance's stories). I reckon that the more people who appreciate and enjoy this unspoiled land, the better it will be protected. So I guess it's all good.

Pushing the crawdad across the ice to Uncle Ted's private island was easy. There was just enough snow over the ice to provide traction without my strap-on boot spikes, and not too much snow for the crawdad to plow through. More importantly, the ice was thick enough to support my 180 pounds without snowshoes. Often you can tell when the ice is "good" by how much it "talks." Groaning, popping, and snapping is an indicator that ice is forming. And Rainbow's ice was "talking" loudly as the low morning sun warmed the temperature into the teens. If I had thought the ice was dicey, I would have strapped-on my snowshoes to spread my weight. But this is controversial among ice travelers because while snowshoes reduce your chances of "going through" the ice, they complicate your ability to climb out if you do. I was glad not to have to worry about such triviality this morning. I just wanted to get this damn roof done so I could go fishing.

After about twenty minutes of mushing, I made landfall at the beach near the boathouse. As a courtesy to my valued customer, I thought I should inspect the outbuildings before wrestling the ladder out of the carriage house. As you can guess, Uncle Ted's shack was only accessible by water, and like many of the quaint dwellings on these private islands, they had their own power-generating plant. Uncle Ted's camp had a beautiful view of Buck Hill in the Debar Mountain Wild Forest. Consequently, his estate was also visible to hikers on Buck Hill, and therefore, the Adirondack Park Agency wouldn't let him install unsightly solar panels or windmills. Never to be deterred, Uncle Ted solved his power problem by installing a high-tech, state-of-the-art propane generator. The camp was closed for the winter, so the genset was in rest mode, but when I inspected the digital readout on the power plant building (disguised to look like an authentic log lean-to), I observed that it had been cycling through its automated maintenance with no errors. Next, I inspected the boathouse. The lake was low, so I ducked under the overhead doors and checked the boats. I knew he stored his classic mahogany Chris-Craft at Spencer Boat Works, so I only had to check on two antique Old Town Canoes that hung upside down in the overhead slings. The professionally restored boats looked stunning with their varnished cedar interior and cane seats. I took the spiral staircase upstairs and checked the wet bar, head, and showers. I found them all winterized correctly. With everything in order, I headed off to the carriage house to get the ladder.

I thought it was extravagant to have a three-stall carriage house (most people call this building a garage) on an island where there are no roads and hence no cars, but Uncle Ted's restored Willys Jeep and utility terrain vehicles needed storage too. Like the boathouse, everything seemed in order, so I hefted the thirty-six-foot fiberglass extension ladder (without crapping my guts out) and carried it over to Great Camp Thady.

Thanks to digging in the feet of the fully extended ladder into the crusty snow, I easily walked it up and placed it gently on one of Thady's highest roof eves. This is the stage of the job where I should rig lines and don a harness, but like most Adirondack locals, I don't, because this is my job security.

What I mean is that many a Great Camp owner has found that if they hire some pleasant-speaking, customer-oriented, highly web-rated non-local contractor (you can't possibly be a true "Adirondack contractor" and have any of these attributes), they receive a significant bill for minimal service. That's because those guys are safety oriented, OSHA-compliant, and properly insured, and they have to charge for all that nonsensical overhead. My compadres and I might not show up when you expect or quit early to go fishing—or not even be available during deer season—but we do a quality job at a reasonable price. That's because working without a net is just one of the normal risks we take from making a living in this rugged land. After all, logging (and nigh on everybody does a bit of that up here) is not a safe profession.

The shoveling was going so well. My plastic shovel (never hire a guy who uses a shovel with a metal edge to *cleah your woof* —it will damage it) was shoving the snow so fast it was shooting past the first-story roof and landing on the ground beyond it. That was awesome because it was one less massive roof that wouldn't need shoveling. But I didn't mind my time on Camp Thady's roof because the view was breahtaking. Where else can a man work under a cobalt blue sky while seeing majestic snow-covered peaks, as the late morning sun warmed him? I thanked God for allowing me to live in his country.

The problem was I underestimated how much the sun had warmed the roof. As I shoved another crap-ton load of snow toward the eve (with sufficient momentum to clear the first-floor roof), I felt my Bean boots slip. I have found over the years that the live rubber of the original LL Bean Maine Hunting Shoe is the best compound for tactile traction on a wet metal roof. But these weren't Maine Hunting Shoes. Instead, they were the cheaper knock-off Bean boots that Marlene had given me for Christmas. Apparently, they had a harder rubber compound that didn't stick as well on the saran-wrap-thin ice that had formed on the eves. As coefficient of sliding friction increased my velocity, I slid toward the edge of the roof. To counter, I immediately splayed my legs and tried to catch screws with the sides of my boots, but Great Camp Thady had "standing-seam" roofing. I remembered, too late, this expensive roofing didn't have exposed screws!

I have no idea if—like the snow I had shoveled—I missed the first-story roof.

CHAPTER 4

I dreamed I was in the woods, at the foundation. I could see it and its surrounds as they must have been in their heyday. A stately log cabin stood proud above the foundation. There was a clearing around the cabin, with stone fences and several crude outbuildings. The cabin was new; its logs were fresh and not grayed by weather. There were fresh green leaves on deciduous trees, and the cabin's moss chinking and its bark roof reflected vibrant color in—what must have been a bright spring sun? I observed a wisp of smoke was rising from the stone chimney of the fireplace. So real was this vision, and yet, I can only describe my presence as a viewpoint, without body or physical structure. From the back of the cabin, a man walked with a hitch, as though he had a bad hip. He wore rough and torn clothing. I could tell that his shirt had once been white and his suspendered trousers were of thick, gray canvas, with substantial patches of a different material at the bend of both knees. His shirt sleeves rolled up to his elbows, exposing the bronzed skin of his muscular forearms. Even from a distance, I could discern his piercing stare and the expression of desperation and anger on his weathered face. In one hand he carried an axe; in the other was an armload of splits. He took both into the cabin and slammed the heavy plank door; its solid sound echoed in the silent woods. I wondered—*why did he take the axe into the cabin?* A short while later, I saw the smoke of the fireplace thicken and become turbulent.

As I looked to the east, I saw the stark summits of Ester and Whiteface mountains. It surprised me that they were entirely treeless. When I looked back at the cabin, night had fallen, and a thick blanket of snow covered its roof and the ground. From the opaque apertures of its windows, the amber glow of oil lamps and the flickering of the fire showed. A large canine walked by the cabin. *Was it a wolf?* It stopped, sniffed the air, and assessed the homestead. After a moment, it padded on, its paws bicycling efficiently in the snow. The scene appeared so warm and inviting that words cannot describe the euphoric and peaceful feeling that had befallen me. I wanted so badly to walk to the warm cabin and knock on that hand-hewn door, but I couldn't move.

I was feeling the cold seep into my presence. I knew something was wrong and that I needed to move. While contemplating my situation, I observed that the night had given way to a sunny winter's day, and the cabin was gone—only its stone foundation remained, just as it had been when I had first viewed it. But there was a creature moving about the piles of rock. At first, I thought it was a weasel by the way it flowed over rocks and logs in pursuit of prey. *But why wasn't it white, as it should have been during winter?* Also, this cat-sized animal with blonde fur and oversized paws was too large for a weasel; maybe it was a pine marten? As I watched, fascinated by the ferret-like creature's blinding speed, it darted toward me, ran up my shirt, and bit my nose! This sharp pain broke my revelry, and I knew it was time to leave this happy place. I expanded, back into my broken body.

I was lying on my back in the snow that, thankfully, was fairly deep from my shoveling. I had no memory of the fall, so I didn't know if I had missed the first-story roof or how I had initially landed. Amazingly, the only pain I felt was at the tip of my nose. I assumed this was frostbite, which meant I had been unconscious for a while. Despite this, I knew I was busted-up pretty bad. Just the act of breathing caused things to rattle and grind in my chest. But I could wiggle my toes and move my hands, so my spinal cord was still communicating with my limbs. This was good news. What was unknown was whether I had fractured any of the vertebrae supporting this neural network—the simple act of moving could sever the cord and leave me paralyzed. This was an unknown risk. But I couldn't stay lying in the snow; freezing was a known risk, so I had to move.

I rolled on to my side. This was difficult because I had frozen into the snow, and when I got unstuck, about three inches of packed snow clung to my back, adding to my weight. This was a real test of my spine's integrity, and it was one that apparently I had passed because I could stand. But my legs were wobbly, and my head ached. After falling thirty feet, I expected this. What I didn't expect was the spray of scarlet blood when I coughed. I could feel loose bones in my chest and back, so I reasoned that one of them must have punctured a lung. My basic understanding of human anatomy and physiology made me realize that this was serious, and I needed to get medical help as soon as possible. I had a cell phone but had left it in the truck because there was no service at Camp Thaddy. However, there was spotty service along the lakeshore, so I needed to make it to the truck while the symptoms of shock and adrenaline were still blocking my pain. Realizing I couldn't push the crawdad, I grabbed a paddle to keep me from going under if I broke through the ice. Besides, I reasoned that since the ice hadn't broken on the way out, it should be okay for the way back, as long as I stayed on my track. As an afterthought, or maybe it was a forethought, I took the towel I kept in the boat, and rolled it around my neck as a support collar. My over-cautious mind was concerned about a hairline crack in one of the cervical vertebrae that would give way if I slipped and fell on the ice. With a chest full of bones rattling around like a box of loose Legos, I set off.

As I reckoned, I had been out for a while but couldn't guess the time of day. This was because, despite the bright winter sun, my view had that eerie twilight gloom, like just after sunset. This vista was familiar because this is the way most of my dreams appear, but now I attributed this obscuring phenomenon to traumatic shock. But at least I could see well enough to find the shoreline.

I got close enough to the shore to see my truck before I "went through." I hadn't counted on the intense afternoon sun degrading the near-shore ice. The good news was that the horizontally held paddle kept me from going completely under, and my cervical vertebrae still had integrity because I could feel the icy cold water right down to the tips of my toes. I wasn't paralyzed. Since I didn't completely submerge, I wasn't sure of the water's depth, but this close to shore I didn't think it would be over my head. Of course, it didn't matter how deep the water was because I couldn't climb out of the water-filled hole I was in. Every time I tried to heave myself up, the ice broke in front of me. At this, I recalled a lesson from a long-ago ice awareness seminar: *Don't try to get out of the water in the direction that you were going—that's likely to be more thin ice. Instead, turn around and attempt to exit from the direction where you came—it held you, once.* So this I did, and in the process of turning around I lost my canoe paddle somewhere under a sheet of ice and discovered that the water was, in fact, over my head. However, the lesson from that seminar was correct; the ice toward my backtrack was solid, but because my previous attempts at self-extrication had splashed water on it, it was also very slippery. My soggy gloves just couldn't get traction on the slick ice. Adding to the problem was that my saturated Carhartt coveralls now weighed about fifty pounds and were pulling me down. In hindsight, I wished that I had packed my ice awls. These simple devices are just a couple of sticks with spikes in them that are joined together with a lanyard which you wear around your neck. If you go through, they provide the purchase needed to pull yourself out of the water and on to, hopefully, good ice. My ice awls were safe, still hanging from a nail in the woodshed. As I exhausted myself by trying to climb out, I thought of another ice awareness lesson that I hoped I'd never have to use: *If you can't climb out of the water, allow your face, preferably a bearded one, to freeze on the ice's surface. This will prevent you from submerging if you lose consciousness and may allow someone to see you and affect your rescue before you succumb to hypothermia.*

That was another very applicable lesson and one that would work because I had a decent beard. I spread my arms and planted the side of my face on the wet ice as I drifted off. Before I lost consciousness, I thought of that damn foundation.

~*~

I awoke at Saranac Lake General Hospital. There was an IV stuck in my right arm, and I was dressed in one of those ridiculous hospital gowns. My headache was gone, but my body felt like... well, like I'd fallen off a cliff. Most disturbingly, I did not know how I had gotten here—my last conscious memory was of the ice shelf I was clinging to. After that, I'd had a lot of bizarre dreams, but they were fading. Just as I was about to test my legs, a doctor opened the curtain and said, "Good, you're awake." I thought it odd that he was dressed in black fatigues and had a distinctive downstate accent as he asked my name, date of birth, and my address. I reasoned that the interrogation was just to confirm that I was "with it," since the staff must have found my wallet and insurance card. The doc told me where I was, and that two ice fishermen had rescued and brought me here.

After I had acknowledged this info, he listed my injuries. "The scans show you have a mild concussion, a broken right clavicle, a broken left scapula, and six broken ribs—three on each side. As expected, you also have frostbite on your nose, fingers, and several toes. Your most severe injury is a pneumothorax, which is why I scheduled you for a medevac to Burlington Trauma Center for treatment."

The last one got my attention, so I asked, "Wait a minute, how am I getting to Burlington?"

The doc said, "Medevac—that's a helicopter ride. It'll only take about twenty minutes."

"Medevac by North Country Life Flight?" I asked.

"Nope, we tried them, but they're busy on a High Peaks rescue. You're going by a private agency," he answered.

To which I replied, "Bullshit! I am not paying thirty thousand dollars for a helicopter ride that I don't even need."

At this, the doc got testy and said, "Mr. Brocke, I don't know if you understand the seriousness of your injury. You have a leaking right lung, and it can collapse, causing a heart attack. That's why Burlington is the best place for your treatment."

I knew he was simplifying things for me, so I said, "Look, Doc, I know the complications of a mediastinal shift, and I also know needle decompression can resolve them before their onset. I also know inserting a chest tube is something any ER tech can do. Hell, even I know how to do it. But I don't think I need a thoracostomy because I'm breathing fine, and I've only had one incident of hemoptysis, and that was before walking for three miles and going through the ice."

After I had finished my tirade, he shrugged and said, "I'll see if the doctor is busy."

Before I could say, "I thought you were a doctor," he left, closing the curtain behind him.

A short while later, a gray-haired gentleman, in a white coat, along with a young lady, dressed in hospital scrubs, opened the curtain. I was reluctant to assign titles to anyone after I had wasted my breath with that last guy, but I was fairly sure he was a real doctor and she was an honest-to-goodness nurse. Imagine my surprise when I discovered that I had their titles reversed!

After the doc briefly listened to my chest, she said, "I think you will be just fine, but you're going to spend the night so we can make sure your lung has healed."

Before she turned to leave, I asked, "What's with my vision? Everything looks dark and brownish—like I'm looking at a negative image."

At this she hastily grabbed a clipboard from the foot of my bed and leafed through a few pages with a furrowed brow. While still reading, she said, "You've suffered a significant cranial deceleration that caused a concussion. Occasionally, this results in ocular bleeding. Your occluded vision is likely the result of blood in the vitreous body. Assuming this doesn't damage your retina, as the aqueous humor exchanges it should reabsorb and your vision will return to normal, over time."

I interpreted her diagnosis as "the whack to my noggin caused my eyes to bleed, and I was looking through blood—that's why everything was sepia toned." *Yuk!*

The doctor left, and while the nurse was fiddling with my IV pump, he said, "We want to stay ahead of your pain and make sure you don't get an infection, so I'm administering some meds through your IV. The pain meds may make you sleepy, so before they take effect, there is someone here who wants to talk with you."

I thought, *Great—Marlene is here! She's probably so glad I'm okay, and hopefully she brought me some proper hospital clothing and my iPad.* Instead, another young lady walked through the curtain, only this one was wearing a sharp black uniform.

I could feel the warmth of the pain meds taking effect as I recognized her attire from my former DEC employment. She was an encon officer. At this, I realized my red retinal filter made her uniform appear black but it was really green. Her official title was environmental conservation officer, the direct descendants of Teddy Roosevelt's fabled game protectors, only now they had evolved into the wilderness police. After she professionally and politely introduced herself as ECO Bridget Fiory, she also kindly asked how I was feeling.

The pain meds were really kicking in; my tongue felt thick and my head got heavy. I didn't want to embarrass myself by talking, so I smiled and nodded like an idiot, although I wondered why she was visiting me. At first, I thought she knew me from my days of working in the Ray Brook office, but she was too young. I didn't have to wait long to find out why she was here.

After her intro and obligatory kindness, she got right to the point. "Mr. Brocke, I am issuing you an appearance ticket for 'not wearing a helmet while operating a snowmobile on the waters of the State.' You are lucky that your injuries aren't more serious. I will also need to verify your registration and insurance information, which I understand you likely won't be able to produce until you recover the machine. Also, not to add to your problems, but you are responsible for recovering the snowmobile. My advice to you is to accomplish this as soon as possible, because if there is any evidence of a petroleum spill or even a sheen of oil on the water, you are subject to a fine of ten thousand dollars a day."

I thought, *These drugs are good*, because I had no friggin' idea what she was talking about. I hadn't owned a snowmobile since 1981. So I waited for her to take a breath, forced my thick tongue to move, and tried to say, "I don't have a snowmobile," but what came out was, *"Ah mon't hab a nomoble."*

Amazingly, she seemed to understand, and redirected. "Then whose snowmobile were you using when you went through the ice?"

What was with the snowmobile? Again I formed an answer, "I wasn't on a snowmobile," which came out as, *"Ah wobbon on ah nobol."*

At this, she put on her best bad cop act, raised her voice, and said, "Is that so, Mr. Brocke? Well, you must think that I'm pretty stupid to believe that nonsense, because I've investigated dozens of snowmobile/ice accidents, and most of the victims exhibit the same injury pattern you have. How else do you explain your injuries, Mr. Brocke?"

When she got nasty, I realized she shouldn't be interrogating me while I was doped up, and anything I said wouldn't be admissible in court. But I had nothing to hide and just wanted to end this because I was getting so sleepy. With my eyes barely open, I said, *"Ah fell off da woof."*

Holy crap, I sounded just like Uncle Teddy!

~*~

I spent that night in the hospital, not that I would have known, or cared. When I awoke, I noticed that Marlene must have stopped by because on my tray was a fresh set of underwear and a T-shirt, along with a note that only said to call her cell when I needed a ride. The following morning they conducted another brain scan as a condition of my release. At about noon the doctor poked her head in my room and loudly proclaimed my head scan revealed "nothing was there." While I didn't appreciate the way she announced the good news, I was glad to get out of sickbay and back to work. Except that I couldn't work, not for at least eight long weeks, because I had a bunch of broken bones in my chest, which needed that long to knit together. To add to the torture, the doc said I'd suffered a mild concussion and that I shouldn't read or watch TV for a few days to de-stress my brain. What the hell was I supposed to do for those days?

I got dressed and called Marlene's cell. After six rings, it went to voicemail. In her most sexy Long Island accent (an oxymoron), Marlene's outgoing message stated that she was likely in a meeting, and to leave a detailed message about the property I was interested in. This was bullshit!

Surprised at how angry this made me, I got a hold of myself and left a message. "Marlene, where the hell are you? Come get me!"

Before I headed to the lobby for what was likely to be a long wait, I thought I should clean up and try to look somewhat presentable. I was absolutely shit-shocked when I looked in the bathroom mirror. I realized then I must have taken a good whack to my noggin because there were huge black semi-circles under both of my eyes. Adding to this ghoulish image was that the tip of my frostbitten nose was black. But even scarier than this was that about half of my beard was missing! They must have had to cut it to extract me from the ice. *But why didn't the hospital staff just shave me, instead of leaving me to look like a jerk?* I looked around for any utensils to cut off the rest of my facial hair and could only come up with my Buck knife. I knew from experience that this would not be sharp enough, plus I hadn't cleaned it after skinning that coywolf I'd shot last month. Resigned that I had no need and was in no mood to impress anyone, I headed to the lobby.

I called again, waited for an hour, called again, and was so pissed-off that I was about to walk when I observed a mirror-black BMW X5 stop at the portico entrance. I was admiring the sharp-looking SUV when its vaguely familiar and equally sharp dark-suited driver hailed me through the partially open passenger window.

"Hello, Mason. Marlene has sent me to pick you up. She's showing a property at Silver Lake and cannot break free." At the sound of his phony English accent, I recognized the guy as Marlene's hoity-toity real estate partner, Frederick St. John.

I'd met him at a few of Marlene's company Christmas parties and had immediately taken a dislike to him. Mainly because I thought he was pretentious (read: faggy) and a pompous ass. But that's not what I really think because I really think he has the hots for Marlene but is too scared of me to do anything about it—which is good for both parties because I wouldn't fare well in Dannemora or any maximum security prison. Frederick also wears these Euro-trendy expensive clothes, has black hair, is clean shaven, and Marlene has told me (repeatedly) that many women think he's handsome. It's a good thing she informed me of this because I think he's butt ugly, but then again, I think most men are. Frederick also stays fit and trim from his daily personal training sessions at the spa, and he's about ten years younger than me, which is probably why he still has black hair. Anyway, to add to Frederick's pompousness, he even pronounces his last name as "Sinjin" instead of St. John—what a douche bag! Additionally, why would anyone with half a brain drive around the

North Country in a $90,000 BMW? Everyone knows the most practical vehicle for these untamed roads is a Jeep, or a Subaru, or an old four-wheel-drive pickup, like mine. Double douche bag!

But with no other option, I mumbled "Thanks, Freddy" (by now you can probably guess why I call him Freddy) and got into his immaculate vehicle. As I opened the passenger door, I noticed that there was a disposable paper floor mat along with a blanket covering the seat, which is why I closed that door and muttered something about needing more room as I scuffed into the unprotected, virgin leather and pristine carpet of the more spacious rear bench seat. I think I may have also said something about feeling nauseous and having explosive diarrhea.

I could tell that Freddy was already nervous about chauffeuring this half-man, half-animal-looking guy with the black nose and eyeshadow when I advised that instead of my home, I needed a ride to my truck, which was still at Rainbow Lake. Since this was farther, it ratcheted-up Freddy's stress level, and he compensated by driving fast, while frequently sneaking peeks at me from his rear-view mirror—probably hoping that I wasn't puking, pissing, or shitting.

There was about a foot of snow covering my truck when Fast Fred hurriedly dropped me off. He also didn't follow the rule of the North by hanging around to see if my truck would start—a triple douche bag! I retrieved my key from the gas filler and creaked open the passenger side door because the driver's side was frozen stuck. As I slid across the torn seat cover, I winced and let out an unintentional moan. This grinding jolt of pain made me realize that I was overdue for my narco pain medicine, which was probably a good thing since I was about to do something that I wasn't supposed to—and that was to drive. And even though I also know you're not supposed to, I stomped on the accelerator pedal a few times before cranking-over the well-run-in V-8. My truck may be old, but it was still fairly reliable, and after a few mournful groans, it popped, coughed, and shook like a wet dog as it rumbled to life, leaving just a trace of blue smoke in the parking area.

Marlene wasn't home when I arrived.

CHAPTER 5

Several long days passed while I convalesced. The good hospital drugs had worn off, and I was feeling a lot more pain than expected. Every part of my body hurt, like one big open wound. I found myself enjoying my pain-med slumber a little too much, so I regularly popped my oxycodone, which kept me asleep and dreaming in the guest bedroom. I slept in this room only because the woodshed was too cold. Since my homecoming, I had not seen Marlene, and a smoldering rage was igniting within me.

Unfortunately, most of my rage was directed at Marlene. I've read that accident victims often blame something to deal with their misfortune. It was easy for me to understand why I could needlessly blame her—it was because of her relationship to Uncle Ted. Deep within, I must have blamed Uncle Ted for hiring me to shovel his roof. *Weird how that works.* Even though I understood the psychology of this misdirected blame, I couldn't stop it. Marlene is smart, and I think she knew this, which is probably why she avoided me. But still, her lack of concern about my injuries and not even being with me at the hospital—that was the last straw in our impassioned but stressed marriage. Despite this, I missed her, and her absence made me realize how alone I felt.

But I remember that it wasn't always this way.

~*~

We'd met when I was taking summer courses at Woods Hole Oceanographic Institution. During that time, I wasn't sure whether I wanted to be a marine biologist or a wildlife biologist, so I studied both. Marlene's parents were generous contributors to the institute, and they were often invited to the campus to see how their money was being spent. That summer, the institute commissioned their newest research vessel, *The Mowat,* which was actually a small, seventy-five-foot ship, and had invited their biggest contributors for a tour and a cruise. Reginald and Darlene Holloway were among the golden plank donors, and they brought their only daughter as a guest. I was working a student job as a deckhand aboard *The Mowatt* on that picture perfect day—complete with a cloudless sky, no wind, and a gentle rolling swell on a deep blue sea. But it wasn't long before the barely noticeable heaving and pitching of *The Mowat* had this very attractive, auburn-haired girl puking her guts out. Apparently, I was the only one who noticed her as she crawled and barfed her way below deck in complete misery. Meanwhile, on the fantail, champagne flowed, and the esteemed guests consumed hors d'oeuvres as the ship steamed on. Seeing an opportunity, I grabbed a washcloth and towel from the head and went to the young lady's aid. Through wretches, she told me that her name was Marlene, and that she hated boats, and water, and just about everything out of doors. I should have paid attention to this back then, but I didn't because I was foolishly listening to my biological reproductive head.

I knew seasickness was from an equilibrium imbalance caused by the brain receiving conflicting signals: while the eyes show a world that is stationary, our body, and in particular the balance sensors in our ears, send signals of a moving environment. I also knew the solution was to synchronize the eyes and ears so the brain could sort the signals out. The best way to do this was to look at the horizon, and the best way to look at the horizon was to steer the boat. So I bought Marlene up to the flying bridge and asked the captain if she could take the helm. The captain must have known who her parents were because he immediately agreed to my request by saying, "Aye, aye, Sir!"

This false deference may have caused the seasick and distraught Marlene to believe I had higher station than that of the captain. Of course, I did nothing to dispel this crazy notion and may have even perpetuated it a little. As I helped Marlene steer, I could tell that she was feeling a lot better and grateful for my intervention. After about a half hour of flirting, I made a show of turning the helm back over to the captain and walked Marlene to the party on the fantail. She introduced me to her parents as the "ship's master." I'm reasonably sure they didn't know what that title meant, but it sounded impressive, so, for the time being, they accepted me enough to grant dating privileges.

CHAPTER 6

Reminiscing was distracting, but it did little to ease my cabin fever. Since I wasn't supposed to read or watch the idiot box, little things, like waiting for the mail, became the highlight of my day when I was awake. One day, a couple of letters came that made me discard medical advice and read them. One was a get-well card from Uncle Teddy, and even though it was addressed to Marlene, I opened it. Along with some well wishes that Marlene was supposed to convey was a check for two hundred dollars which, surprisingly, was made out to me. Good old Uncle Ted, he must have watched my tumble on his SatCam because I'm pretty sure that Marlene hadn't called to tell him of the sad, sad news. But I appreciated his check, and it reminded me to follow-up with the guy I had hired to stow Uncle Ted's ladder. I had to hire this mutt because I knew I shouldn't and couldn't lift the heavy ladder, so it was fifty bucks well spent.

The second letter was from the college stating that enrollment for Adirondack Biology 101 was closed due to an overwhelming response. *These kids today—they just couldn't wait to bump up their GPA with subsidized camping, dope smoking, and spawning!* The college board also stated they would assign an assistant to help me with the course. The translation: since the course was a success, they were replacing this lowly adjunct professor with a real one, and I would be their trainer. I realized this would probably be my last class unless they invited me to be an unpaid "volunteer assistant" instructor. My answer to that opportunity would be from the phonetic alphabet I used during my tour of duty in the army: November-Foxtrot-Whiskey (No Frigging Way). With that thought, I vowed to make my last class the best one ever.

As the walls continued to close in, I skipped a pain-med cycle so it would be safe for me (and for everyone else) to drive. Besides, I learned that plain old Motrin worked almost as well as the narcotic stuff, and it didn't make me sleepy.

Now, any person in their right mind would have been happy just to drive around and see the mountains, but not me; I knew where I had to go—to look for that damn foundation! The ER doc said walking was good for me, but I think she meant walking around the house or maybe on a silly sidewalk or something. I figured that walking through the woods on snowshoes was about the same as walking anywhere else, just as long as I didn't fall.

I considered the weight of my pack though. I kept my everyday "woods" kit stocked with all the necessities for spending a quiet night in the woods during a blizzard, just in case I got a mite bewildered (read: lost, and this happens more often these days). But I also knew the heft of the pack suspended by shoulder and sternum straps would surely make it impossible for me to carry. So I downloaded all that I could cram into my smaller butt-pack. I took my first aid kit (consisting of a blood-clotting agent and a tourniquet), a topo map and compass, waterproof matches, and para-cord. I wrapped it all in my old army poncho, which I could rig as an emergency shelter. As an afterthought, I threw in a small baggie of GORP (Good Old Raisins and Peanuts) for emergency food. I also thought about taking my grampa's Colt revolver, but instead opted for his old tomahawk. I'd usually pack both, but carrying weight was a consideration for my decrepit body, and since they weighed about the same, I took the hatchet—just in case I needed to make a shelter. I know that most people would consider it excessive to pack all this gear for just a walk in the woods. But like the old Adirondack guides used to say when their clientele complained about the enormity of supplies they would make them pack-in: "You can walk into the woods without them, but you just might not walk out again."

I was pleasantly surprised that despite passing time and the snow that had fallen since my last shed-searching expedition, I could still find evidence of my previous tracks. The mid-morning sun revealed the slightest depression upon the nearly perfect blanket of powder, which I followed as if it was a homing beacon vectoring me to my target. Also, I was glad I was wearing traditional bear-paw snowshoes because they were keeping me up well, especially when I stayed on my previous tracks. The rawhide bear paws didn't have integrated crampons like modern synthetic snowshoes, so they weren't much good for mountaineering, but you couldn't beat 'em for keeping you up in deep snow. Although, as the melting snow softened their leather harnesses, they would stretch, allowing me to occasionally step out of a shoe and step into testicle-deep snow. I reckon that just as everything in life is a compromise, my antique bear paw's superior floatation was offset by the pain-in-the-ass of constantly having to tighten their leather harnesses as you trekked. As such, I had to make three adjustments and even had to make a couple of new holes in their straps. But in the end, it was worth it, because, after a few miles, I was looking down into the foundation.

Frankly, I was amazed at how easily I had found it this time. I had searched for the foundation several times under the pretext of shed-hunting but had walked in circles and even become a mite bewildered. I wondered again if there was an iron ore deposit in the area so I could blame this anomaly for causing my compass to drift. The entrepreneurs of the previous century knew the Adirondacks were loaded with iron. The only thing that saved this hallowed ground from becoming a six million acre mining pit was a contaminate that made the smelting of Adirondack ore unprofitable during those days. Decades later, that contaminate was discovered to be titanium! Luckily, by the time we discovered how valuable the element was, laws prohibiting unregulated mining were in place. *I'm glad I live in a park!*

This time, when searching for the foundation, I followed one of my previous tracks, but I also used a little intuition and terrain assessment to look for where I would build a cabin in these woods. After about a mile straight in, I kept walking up a gentle slope until I descended. Knowing that flash flooding and mudslides were serious threats for the early settlers, I kept to the high ground. I walked in a decreasing spiral pattern until I reached the center of the plateau—which is where I found it!

This was, in fact, a fine place for a cabin. It had commanding views of the Stevenson Range, and along its ridge, I could discern the peaks of Whiteface, Ester, and Magic mountains. For what it was worth, the surrounding land was level and plowable. Within my line of sight from the foundation was a sizable pond—a water source and another necessity of life. Living here would have been hard, but it would have been living in extreme beauty.

The wind was kicking up, and since I had ceased vigorous activity, the trapped sweat that my expensive Gore-Tex parka hadn't dissipated was chilling me. Also, I had shaved my half-beard and was surprised how much it (that is, the full beard) had kept me warm. With no protective fur, the wind froze the frost that clung to my stubble, forming a white beard of ice; but at least I was wearing a nose muff so that part wouldn't refreeze and get freezer burn. Wanting to escape the piercing wind, I descended into the protected and warm womb of the foundation.

Just like my last foray into the foundation, I was amazed by how little snow was on the floor—only a dusting covered a thick carpet of deciduous leaf and pine needle litter. I shuffled to the approximate center of the pit, once again trying to estimate its dimensions. As I did this, I began to feel nauseated and lightheaded. I was getting dizzy as well and caught myself just before stumbling on some obstacle underfoot. When

I looked up, through blurred vision, the foundation walls had moved farther away and the surrounding trees had faded. I needed to get a hold of myself, climb out, and try eating snow while I could still swallow. My excessive walking must have caused internal bleeding, and I needed to hydrate and head back before I could no longer move. But before I did, I had the dream-like feeling of falling as the ground beneath my feet disappeared, and I sank into a deep crevasse. *Had I been unlucky enough to discover an Adirondack sinkhole?*

I say I descended into the crevasse rather than fell because I drifted downward as the surrounding scenery changed from snowy, organic vegetation to barren, solid rock. Upon reaching the bottom of the pit, I surveyed my situation. I was at the bottom of a steep, rock-walled crater. I estimated the surface to be at least fifty feet above my head—but I had no head, or body. I realized I was in that remote-viewing, dreamy confusion, like I had experienced during my previous vision of the foundation —only this seemed terrifyingly real. Was I a spectator of this dynamic scene, or a participant? *But of what, where, and... when?*

It's funny the things you notice when you're crap-in-your-pants scared—the doc was right about my vision clearing. Gone was the dim reddish-brown monochrome, and it was replaced by a flood of bright vibrant color. Everything was so detailed —I could even see bluish-green veins in the granite as if I was viewing the scene in high-def. Even more amazing was I could perceive things I couldn't see, as though a narrator was describing it to me.

As I looked upward at the rim of the crater, I observed that the clear sky had a greenish hue, but it was fading to black as fiery debris rained down from it. Great clouds of inflammable ash floated from above, appearing like snowflakes from hell. I sensed searing heat from all around and felt significant tremors accompanied by the sound of continuous thunder. Beneath me, deep cracks appeared. As I peered into their depths, I saw a glowing red—*was that magma?* Since I was crap-in-my-pants scared, I willed myself to wake up, but I couldn't snap out of this trance. Whatever had befallen me wasn't done, and I wasn't just caught in a daydream. I was trapped in a nightmare.

The scene flickered like an old silent movie, and its frequency appeared to be increasing. Something within me understood that this represented the passage of days and that I was witnessing past geologic events, only in ultra-fast-forward time. This precipitous transition of day and night illuminated the scene with an eerie twilight shade. If I concentrated, I could discern the sun, and intermittently, the moon's passage across the sky, but I would miss dozens of sunrises with a single blink. The moon was the easiest to spot because it occurred only after the crossing of twenty-eight suns, and it also appeared twice its normal size. I noticed that the greenish sky had returned, but angry black clouds were forming.

In a moment, clouds of steam occluded the darkened sky as thick, gray, ash-laden raindrops poured from it. Through the steam, I could see water cascading down the walls of the pit, and it wasn't long before it filled, causing my viewpoint to float above its surface. What I saw was an unfamiliar, barren landscape, shadowed by jagged mountains. My inner narrator told me that most of these stark bluish-gray spires, many of them as tall as Everest, would not survive the onslaught of what was to come. The coming glaciers would pulverize them, and those that remained would become Whiteface, Algonquin, Marcy, and the other High Peaks.

As the torrential rains continued, I observed that the swelling flood waters had reached the foot of these mountains, which were now becoming vibrant green with moss. As I watched, lush vegetation and palm trees formed at the water's edge. *Were those jungles?* I could sense that this humid atmosphere contained very little oxygen. Photosynthesis would have to work for thousands of years before the land could support fauna. I glimpsed at the pale blue sky, its greenish hue having evaporated as I unwillingly submerged back into the murky water of the pit. Something told me that this was saltwater, and it was teeming with much more than pond life. I saw various forms of mollusks littering the seabed, and primitive shelled creatures rattled as they swam by. These invertebrates looked like the predecessors of trilobites, but I saw no fishes. As the seconds passed, I observed a meter-long sea scorpion pursuing a fully-evolved trilobite in a primordial predator-prey chase. A moment later, the sea receded, and I looked up at the crater's rim, anticipating the next apocalypse that something destined me to behold.

Along with the barely perceptible flicker, there was now a pulsing contrast of the sky's hue and brightness. Intuition told me that our Earth had just tilted on its axis, and I was watching the annual changing of the seasons, only at about a hundred times per second. The ground shook, and an abysmal subterranean rumbling ensued; simultaneously, I sensed a deep, penetrating chill. The rim of the crater became covered with a sheet of opaque ice that I sensed was at least a mile thick. But the ice was rapidly sliding by, and as it did, it ground away at the crater's rim, raining rubble into its depth. At this, I recalled the story of the iceman of the alps, and how his corpse had survived and was preserved, perfectly intact, for thousands of decades. Similar to my predicament, he had fallen into a crevasse, was frozen, then dehydrated and spared the pulverizing effect of alpine glaciers that covered his grave until climate change caused their recession and uncovered his tomb. *Was this my fate, to be preserved as the "iceman of the Adirondacks"?* Every so often, I saw a boulder the size of a house suspended scores of feet above, trapped in the crystal-clear ice. These enormous rocks floated by as if they were tiny pebbles being pushed down a stream. After several minutes, which I realized represented a hundred thousand years of geologic time, the ice melted, leaving the crater filled with water and substantially reduced to what would be its depth for the next several hundred millennia.

The scene faded back to sepia tone.

I awoke, still standing in the foundation but in partial darkness. Through the light cloud cover, I observed a crescent moon that appeared to be its normal size. In the distance, I heard the haunting howl of coywolves, and I knew I had returned to the present.

~*~

I was lucky that my green headlamp was still in my kit because I needed it to avoid the face-swatting, eye-poking, hat-stealing branches along my track back, not that I would have noticed or cared. I was still shaking when I got to the truck and even forgot to say my "please start" prayer before firing her up. I needed a drink to sort this out, so I stopped at the Downtowne Grille before heading home.

After my second pint of Leaning Pine (a local and fairly high-octane brew), I took stock of my situation. I was still recovering from a concussion, but would a brain bruise have given me the vivid visions I had experienced? It could, but I knew this was unlikely, as most people recover from a concussion without such incidents. Equally unlikely was that it was some sort of hallucination from my narco-pain meds, as I hadn't taken any since yesterday. Besides, they were mere opioid-acetaminophen combos, and more likely to cause drowsiness, not delusions. This was something else. I deduced that my vision was of an Adirondack prehistorical period, something of which I hadn't studied and consequently knew little of. I would solve that by going to the Saranac Lake Free Library tomorrow. They had an excellent reference section consisting of an entire floor that was even staffed with a historian-librarian. That would, at the very least, be a good start.

It surprised me that the Downtowne Grille was empty and yet they were still open. That was odd for an Adirondack business because they operate on such narrow margins—if they're not busy, they're losing money. Without regard, I left a twenty on the bar by my empty glass for the inattentive bartender and headed out the back door. *Maybe she'd remember me the next time*

I stopped in?

Marlene wasn't home when I arrived.

~*~

The following morning, I headed to the library. I was lucky that the streets were clear and traffic was light because I was definitely guilty of distracted driving since my thoughts were jumbled and filled with emotion as I tried to sort yesterday's events. One of those emotions was fear. That is, I was afraid that my tup off of Uncle Ted's roof had done a bit more to my brain than the mild concussion that the MRI had shown. What if I had a permanent, traumatic brain injury, and this would be my life —never knowing when I was going to lapse into unreality to be tortured with these apocalyptic, nightmarish visions! I had to make sense of this, and the first step would be to determine if what I saw was actual prehistory or just a random misfiring of my brain's synapses.

While a small part of me was glad to not see Marlene last night, a bigger part wished that I had someone to talk to about this. Of course, I knew sharing my transcendental experience with Marlene was my sure ticket to an involuntary vacation at the Tupper Lake Sanitarium, known as the "Nervous Hospital" by the locals. So, in retrospect, I was lucky that she wasn't home because being so confused, I'm sure I would have spilled my guts. Actually, I don't think Marlene came home at all last night. But then again, I couldn't be sure because I had taken one of my narco-pain pills after pre-medicating with a couple of those high-octane beers. Consequently, I was out like a light, and thankfully, I didn't even dream.

The main level of the library was nearly empty, and the downstairs history section was completely empty. While I was glad not to have to fight traffic on the way over (rush hour traffic in Saranac Lake can be almost as busy as that of a small village), and equally glad not to have a crowd at the library (sometimes there are upwards of five or six people milling around and quietly reading), I was wondering where the heck everyone was—*skiing, maybe?* I tried to but couldn't imagine the library's wizened historian shushing down Whiteface. Then it occurred to me—it was Winter Carnival Week! Everyone was probably hanging out at the ice palace down by the lake. The brave volunteers of the community, along with the help of inmates from one of the local prisons, had built a beauty this year. For the last few winters, it's been touch-and-go whether there would even be enough ice on Lake Flower to harvest for making the palace, as the building block of the castle requires at least eight inches of solid, clear ice, which they cut using traditional ice handsaws. Talk about a scary job—that's chilling! I had an involuntary shiver as this thought brought back the terrifying image of those ice age glaciers scraping over my head. Without regard, I started my unaided search by pawing through the books of the geology section. For comparison, I brought my notes from Dr. Torrance's AB 101 class. Although many of his most poignant history lectures were given around the campfire, the yellowed, dog-eared composition notebook from 1972 still had the notes from most of his lessons—many of them scribbled by firelight.

My cryptic notes indicated that one of the good doctor's first lectures was about Grenville rocks, but it must have been one of those "campfire" sessions because my notes were indecipherable. Aided by a rolling ladder, I searched the upper shelf of the ceiling-high bookcase until I found a book entitled *The Geologic History of the Grenville Period*. It was big and dusty, with big words and printed in microprint way back in 1949. Fortunately, I'm used to reading wildlife study papers from that era. After reading too much about Grenville rock strata—which are the oldest rocks in the world, formed when the Earth was still a molten ball—I skipped to a section about the Laurentian system. I read that Grenville rocks compose the core of the Adirondack landscape. Newer rock (relatively newer) was the molten "anorthosite," which pushed up through the Grenville strata to create the High Peaks of this region—only they were a lot higher when they first formed, many of them taller than those of the

Himalayas. Because of anorthosite's heat-forged density, when it cooled it formed a coarse-grained, bluish-gray stone that became the foundation of the Adirondack Mountains before glacial erosion, sedimentation, and vegetation made them what they are today. *Holy shit—I saw this happen!*

But what about that green sky, the jungles, the seascape, and all that ice? To determine if this was real, I would have to scan through about a dozen natural history books only to find that my vision had validity. And what I discovered, as they say up here, was weird.

At each revelation, I compared what I read in the reference books to the more intelligible scribblings in my notebook. Turns out, Dr. Torrance had said it all; I just had forgotten it after the test. I made fresh notes, summarizing the resolutions to my queries:

Because of extensive volcanic activity, Earth's first atmosphere was composed of methane. Thus, the greenish sky. (I was grateful for not being able to smell during my vision.)

When the water suspended in this new atmosphere condensed, it fell and formed the Earth's first oceans. Plant life was the first to colonize the land, the process of this being much like it is today: primitive forms of lichen grew on bare rock, creating acids that would, over eons, break the rock down into mineral soil. More advanced plants, like mosses and eventually ferns, would grow and die on the newly formed soil, thus creating an organic layer capable of supporting a rain forest type of flora—a jungle.

While the plant life was forming on land, deep within this ancient ocean that covered most of the planet, single-celled life forms were developing in the nutrient-rich organic soup of this saline water. In fact, the chemistry of this sea would be the basis for all fish, reptilian, and mammalian blood. Mollusks and other filter feeders were the first to develop and manipulate this environment to pave the way for more advanced life. During this period, trilobites and scorpions, the ancestors of insects, would later move to the land. But they would be the climax of this aquatic ecosystem because there wouldn't be time for fish to evolve—the ice was coming.

Over millions of years, the photosynthesis of these lush jungles reduced the carbon in the atmosphere and reduced its protective "greenhouse effect." This, combined with a younger and cooler sun of about two million years ago, created unprecedented glaciation, which was the last Ice Age. The most recent of these glacial periods ground away at the Adirondack Mountains for about 10,000 years. This was more than enough time to round them off and deposit the huge boulders from their peaks all around the region.

This was it. I had witnessed the formation of the Adirondacks, but why?

~*~

The discovery that my vision was based in reality and not merely a flight of fantasy made me feel slightly better, but why had I experienced this prehistoric geology lesson? A part of me believed that the experience was location-specific to the foundation. Actually, I hoped this more than I believed it. In a half-assed experiment, I decided to avoid the location for at least a week, just to confirm my suspicion. And to be honest, this was going to be easy because I was scared as hell to go back to the foundation.

CHAPTER 7

The days went by as I healed. Spring was coming, and buckets hung from many sugar maples. I passed the time in my garage, fixing my truck, sharpening my chainsaws, and chucking wood into the woodstove. I loved the ambiance and the feel of wood heat and had briefly considered installing the stove in our home's fireplace, but Marlene wouldn't hear of it. She believes wood is filthy and only poor people use this primitive method of heating—even though wood is the primary heat source for most homes up here. *Well, maybe she has a point?* It was too bad because the old logwood stove would have melded well with our old home's architecture, for there used to be one in every lumberjack bunkhouse, which is what this house used to be.

When I first transferred to Ray Brook, we lived in an apartment in Saranac Lake. I enjoyed living in the quaint, picturesque little village, but Marlene wanted to buy a home on Mirror Lake. But since all of those lakefront properties are listed in the millions, I tried to talk her into a place with mountain views. I know that many of these are almost as expensive as waterfront properties, but I found this old lumber camp with a bunkhouse that was still standing. It was listed as a short-sale, and during the winter, when the trees are leafless, you can see a mountain...sort of. Besides, as I've explained to Marlene (hundreds of times), you've got to be careful when you cut trees and clear your property up here. That's because if you can see a lake or a mountain from your house, you get slapped with a "view tax." Being a Realtor, I'm fairly certain Marlene already knows this.

As I mentioned, it was an old lumberjack camp, where they used to bunk after a hard day of swinging the axe in the Northwoods. While I had to do a little fixing up, this ranch-style house is an easy-to-maintain dream. The inside has an open architecture with rough-sawn board paneling, complete with a kitchen on one end and a fireplace at the other. Near to the bunkhouse was a rather nice two-stall outhouse, and if you guessed that Marlene made me tear it down and install a bathroom inside the house, complete with a jetted hot tub, you'd be right. On the wide-plank flooring, in between the kitchen and the fireplace, are holes where the bunks were once bolted—there were twenty-four of them, twelve sets of bunk beds on each side. The place must have stunk with so many unbathed, tobacco-smoking, bean-farting men sleeping in one house. My sense of nostalgia wouldn't allow me to remove twelve sets of ringed pad eyes that oppose each other along each wall. This is where the lumberjacks would string a rope across the house and hang their socks to dry. Often, Marlene would remind me how "woodchucky" these things looked. But since I haven't heard this word for a while, I think she's given this fight up. Anyway, that useless and drafty fieldstone fireplace would sure look good with a woodstove stuck into it. But there's no need to risk a hernia by moving that hunk of cast iron now.

While I still own this property, we don't live here anymore. Although I still use the garage for my workshop, the house sits abandoned and with its plumbing winterized, especially that damn overpriced hot tub. This is because I inherited another house that actually has mountain views. And, amazingly, even though it's off the grid, Marlene likes it better than the lumberjack bunkhouse. This is probably because it's an original native log cabin and undoubtedly allows her to have "Realtor bragging rights." The Adirondack Life-reading downstate crowd goes nuts for ramshackle places if they have historical origins. I thought the bunkhouse had plenty of history, but apparently not enough. So I had to rig alternative energy with solar and wind to power the satellite internet and the cellular booster, but it works well enough for this little cabin.

Marlene does not know the tumultuous history of this little cabin and would crap her expensive designer leggings if I told her—especially if I divulged my connection with it. I'm sure she would have me committed in "the nervous hospital" if I told her all of it—and maybe that should be so. Again, I'm getting ahead of myself.

While puttering around in the garage one morning, I heard the phone ring. I still keep an old-fashioned landline here, with a loud bell-ringer because, as the locals say, "them little phones don't work up here." I was surprised it was Pug, a local contractor, and he was offering me a deck project over to Loon Lake. Actually, I wasn't too surprised because no local contractor wants to waste his time during the short Adirondack construction season building a deck. That's because, unlike a boathouse, deck additions have narrow profit margins. Also, in contrast to a boathouse, a properly built deck will last practically forever. Whereas, the thick ice on these lakes destroy boathouses quicker than a woodpecker bores holes in pine siding. But city people don't know this, and they like the summer custom of having cocktails on the upper deck of their boathouses, so every spring, they pay to have them repaired— year after year. The wintertime ice provides a springtime income for many intrepid locals by doing what they call "drift-wood pick'n'." This task involves precariously canoeing the fast-flowing lake outlets and retrieving the cedar and pressure-treated skirting that the ice has removed from the boathouses. Then it's sold back, at a discount, to local contractors for the annual pre-Memorial Day repairs. It's a green and low carbon foot-printed seasonal occupation that's good for the local economy. Of course, contractors don't discount anything, and they invoice the recycled skirting as new material. Yep, boathouses are a contractor's dream, and getting a contract to build one is like winning the Adirondack Powerball.

I never get boathouse jobs, and this year, even if I did, I wouldn't be able to do one. That's because I'm still patching up, and the unofficial rule up here is "contractors must complete all camp construction projects by Memorial Day." That rule exists so the hard-working city people can enjoy the fruits of their overpriced camp improvements during that long weekend. Woe betides the local contractor who doesn't afford his client these bragging rights during the official start of the tourist season. With my injuries, I'd be cutting this job close, but the deck was ground level, and it wasn't a big one. So I said yes to Pug, and he sent me the address along with the sketch.

~*~

After a little meandering on some seasonal camp roads, I found the place. It was an incredibly tall A-frame, with a third-story balcony that had a beautiful view of the lake but wasn't on the waterfront. I often wonder why people build such things —what a waste of space—but that's the trade-off for simulating a tree house. Perhaps it's our evolutionary arboreal roots that made this form of architecture popular? Near as I could tell from the sketch was that they wanted the deck built right over an existing concrete patio. That was good—no need for me to pour footers! I'm guessing that they just didn't like the looks of the worn and cracked concrete and they liked staining wood. If they were my clients, I'd talk to them about refinishing the patio with a low-maintenance stamped-concrete facade—it can even be finished to look like marble, brick, or cobblestone. But these were Pug's clients, and frankly, I'm glad that the project was using plain-old native cedar because I wasn't healed up enough for concrete work yet. I took measurements and jotted some notes for my shopping list.

On the way back, I had this overwhelming compulsion to stop at Moose Pond and hike over to the foundation. My scientific experiment wasn't yet complete with only a few days having passed since my Precambrian history lesson, but I had had no hallucinations since. And even though I was still scared shitless about repeating that experience, something stronger than fear was motivating me as I shifted the old Dodge into four-wheel drive for the ascent up the unplowed Moose Pond Road. I reminded myself that I hadn't planned on interior hiking as I tried to talk myself out of this foolishness, but that didn't hold —for in the truck was my pack, snowshoes, and an axe. I had this stuff with me because this is the minimum kit that any-one, with any sense, keeps in their vehicle when driving in the North Country. We carry this stuff because you never know if you must chop through a massive white pine that's blocking the road, or if you'll get buried in an avalanche, or maybe you'll just break down and have to hoof it to home. Lately, breaking down has been foremost in my mind with my heritage (read: old) ve-hicle, but I had nearly every tool I owned with me (except my welder). So I had everything I needed—except courage.

I found the foundation quickly as if it had a homing beacon. I cautiously walked the perimeter, fortifying myself as I paced. The forest was peaceful. There was a light coating of powder over a foot-deep base of crusty March snow. The air was fresh and still. A cloudless cobalt sky highlighted the knobby buds that were showing from the red shoots of the birch trees. A raven croaked as it flew overhead, and with great trepidation, I descended into the abyss.

CHAPTER 8

W hen I reached the foundation's proximal center, I assumed a statue-like stance, waiting for the tumultuous earthshaking and the violent volcanic eruptions of my past viewing experience. I stood still and waited, and then, when I was about to quit, I waited a little longer, until I was both bored and cold. It wasn't happening, and I felt relief, foolishness, and maybe a little let down as I ambled, shuffling through leaf litter, toward the rubble ramp of the fireplace. It occurred to me that my past experience was a dream, a subconscious recollection of Dr. Torrance's fireside lesson of thirty years ago. Some stray millivolt of electrical current must have touched the area of my brain where that lecture was stored, and I lived it instead of merely remembering it. How stupid of me to believe I could have experienced paranormal time transcendence or any other psycho-babble bullshit. The brain was just a computer, and sometimes its operation system hiccuped or farted, and our reality altered. As I climbed out of the foundation, my vision brightened and I noticed that all the snow had melted.

The forest had changed as well. Gone were most of the deciduous trees and in their place were thick woody vines with long needles projecting from their trunks and from their many short branches. This twenty-foot-tall flora resembled the club-moss that covers the shady areas of the forest floor—only now they were trees. *Was I again reliving a forgotten college lecture via remote viewing?* As I contemplated this, my view moved toward an opening in the woods, and I observed a lake where I recalled a vernal pond had been. Something huge was moving through the water and making a substantial wake, the resulting waves lapping along a muddy shore. I focused on the source of the disturbance; it was a large animal. Actually, what I saw was just the beast's head—*a bear swimming in the lake, perhaps?* That was my thought until I saw the creature climb out of the water, and I witnessed the largest beaver ever known to man—the giant beaver. These eight-foot-long aquatic rodents were long extinct, and their offspring had evolved into nearly identical-looking, compact animals of less than one-quarter of this size. That's why the pond had become a lake—this super-sized beaver had dammed it up with those twenty-foot-tall vines. Absolutely amazing.

My view continued beyond the lake to a brushy clearing. The pasture it formed was a riverine valley from the lakeshore to the summits of what I guessed would become the Stevenson Ridge. As I watched, I saw several large elephant-like animals lumbering along a river that split the valley. They appeared to be a large subspecies of an Asian elephant, except they were fur covered and their tusks were much longer and nearly straight. *Were they mastodons?* As I watched, one of these elephants rammed a spruce with its tusk, effortlessly knocking it over. Soon, the other members of the herd gathered and browsed on what had been the top of the fallen tree.

Again my view changed back to the crater of the foundation, but now it was filled with water—*a kettle lake.* I was getting used to not having control of my vista and reasoned that something of great importance was being revealed. This prehistoric spectator also noticed the light had faded to twilight and had that same, barely perceptible, silent film flicker as my first adventure. I observed the dimness fluctuation flashing by as time rapidly advanced. As I watched, the kettle lake drained, or evaporated, leaving sandy sediment lining its floor. After this, my view changed back to the riverine valley as normal daylight returned and the scene stabilized. Gone were the mastodons and in their

place were their successors—the towering, slope-backed creatures I recognized as wooly mammoth. They were magnificent
animals, with great curved tusks, and on the largest one the
tips of them crossed over ten feet in front of its head. Unlike
mastodons, the mammoths moved with grace as they grazed on
riverbank grasses. I recognized that this must have been a family group, comprising a matriarch with three younger offspring.
Since the calves were of varying sizes, I reasoned they were each
separated by several years. The smallest one must have been a
young-of-the-year, even though it was the size of a mature Afri-
can elephant.

From the bush came a fury of activity as three large canines cut the smallest mammoth off from the herd. I realized
these were the hyper-carnivores classified as dire wolves. They
were the progenitors of the modern wolf—only about one-
third larger and robustly endowed with long fangs protruding
from their closed jaws. I recalled that these wolves had the
strongest crushing bite of any canine to date and that they had
specifically evolved to prey on large herbivores. But as herbivores progressed to become swift and agile—like the deer—dire
wolves became extinct because they did not have the social in-
telligence for coordinated hunting. Therefore, it was unlikely
that these three wolves were members of a pack and instead
were probably another family group. As I observed the attack,
a loud trumpeting ensued from the matriarch as she charged
the wolves, but unlike the mastodon, her curved tusks were
nearly useless as weapons, for they had evolved for feeding.
Despite their impressive appearance, evolution shaped them
to strip bark from trees and uncover moss from under deep
snow. All but one wolf deftly avoided her thrusts as they tore
into the juvenile mammoth. The unlucky wolf emitted one last
yelp as the matriarch pinned it to the ground with her tusks,
bearing down with tons of mass. But the matriarch continued
pummeling the lifeless carcass, stuck in some behavioral loop,
completely ignoring the dying throes of her calf. Similarly, the

remaining two wolves feasted on the calf without regard for their lost family member. Apparently, the high-order behaviors of situational thinking and synergistic coordination had not yet evolved.

Again, time advanced, but not significantly, as only several hours seemed to have flashed by. The mammoths had disappeared, and the fully gorged dire wolves lounged by the half-eaten calf carcass, guarding their kill while awaiting their appetite to return. Then, from behind me, came a blood-curdling roar. Something big was coming because I could feel the ground shake as it ran toward my reference point. As the wolves alerted, they looked toward the source of the ferocity and darted off into the bush, abandoning their next meal without even a fight. *What was coming must be the most fearsome of all Pleistocene predators.*

As the creature passed, I observed what appeared to be a super-sized, eight-foot-tall shaggy canine moving with feline agility. Long, thickly muscled limbs pounded the ground as it ran, carrying an equally lean, muscular body of at least a thousand pounds, but its stout head was familiar—it was the extinct short-nosed bear. I remember reading a research paper proposing that this formidable carnivore was more of a scavenger than a predator, like the bears of today. Except the short-nosed bear evolved as a ferocious fighter with tremendous size and an impressive ability to remove other predators from their kills. It could even steal a sabre-toothed cat's quarry. Its demise was because it remained a fervent carnivore, unlike its descendant, the omnivorous black bear. When the meat became scarce, it couldn't switch food sources, and it starved. I was thinking that I should look up the authors of that research paper and confirm their findings, but I filed the thought as time advanced again, and my view returned to the foundation.

Only now the crater was covered with what I believed was an entanglement of blown-down trees, but upon closer inspection, the covering appeared to be deliberately constructed of sticks, bark, and moss—like a bird's nest. As I observed, another anomaly became apparent—it was on fire. Smoke arose from a hole in the center of the morass.

~*~

I awoke, standing on the opposite side of the foundation. Meaning I must have been walking around during my viewing, oblivious to the actual surroundings, and that's dangerous. The other thing that's dangerous is that I must have been doing this for several hours because now it was dark—and cold. At least my time wasn't wasted, for I had lived through the entire Pleistocene epoch in those few hours. But now I had to make my way out of the woods, sans green headlamp, and hoping my truck would start. We were having what the meteorologists call "a late Alberta clipper," but up here we just call this mighty cold weather. Without regard, even though I didn't have a thermometer I knew it must be about twenty below zero because the trees were popping and cracking as the frost froze their sap and caused many of their trunks to split. This was what we North Country folk call "the cleansing cold" because it kills off so many of those pesky invasive insects like emerald ash borers and deer ticks that carry the Lyme disease. But over the past years we haven't had nearly as many of those days below zero as we used to, so Lyme disease is up here, and regrettably, many of us have contracted it. But still, thanks to these nut-shriveling cold days, I take solace because I'm not likely to be attacked by Mexican killer bees anytime soon. Now I wish that I had bought the truck a new battery as I was thinking about… last fall. But like everything, batteries are expensive up here, and it's hard to buy new and costly things for an old truck. I never know when the ol' rig will crap out entirely and waste a good part. At least the night was still, and there was a crescent moon to guide me. But as I walked through the cacophony of splitting wood, there was another sound in the woods, and it was even louder than the snapping trees. An eerie, piecing howl announced the coy-wolves were tracking me!

After witnessing the way those dire wolves had torn that juvenile mammoth apart, I felt the ass-puckering primal fear that prey must feel, even though I knew it was unwarranted. My studies had taught that the northeastern coyote, which is their proper name, is a hybrid of the Canadian grey wolf and the western coyote. This cross-breeding occurred when the western coyote made its eastward geographic migration and avoided population centers by migrating northward, through Canada. Up here, most folks call them coydogs, which is incorrect because although a coyote/dog hybrid is possible, one would not survive for long in the north. That's because domestic dogs go into estrous during the summer. This is lousy timing for survival in the wild because coydog pups would be born during the middle of winter, when food is scarce and conditions are harsh. On the other hand, wolves and coyotes have this figured out, as their estrous period is in the fall. Consequently, a coywolf's pups are born during the spring, thus giving them three seasons of training before the inhospitable winter sets in. The eastern coyote is a wolf-sized canine that is about one-third larger than a western coyote, which is why the uninformed think they are a dog hybrid. Coywolves are successful in the Adirondacks because they did not inherit the social behavior or pack hunting skills of their wolf ancestors. Pack hunting is beneficial for taking down large prey, like moose (or mammoths). But hunting in a pack is a disadvantage when large prey isn't available because the energy spent to take down the quarry has to feed the entire pack, a dinner for up to twelve, for which the largest North Country white-tailed deer would be inadequate. The Adirondack coywolf "gets on" in the north because it preys mostly upon small game, mice, and the occasional fawn, but not moose because there just aren't enough up here—yet.

You'd think all of this useless knowledge would have calmed my ass down as I trekked out of the woods, but when I heard their excited yelps on each side of me it had the opposite effect. I realized they were herding me. Likewise, I should have felt assured knowing this was a family group of coywolves hunting me instead of a pack; at least Mom and Dad were doing something fun with the kids. Nonetheless, this did little to assuage my fear as I caught moonlit glimpses of their long, lean bodies darting through the spruce thickets alongside me. It surprised me at how mangy these typically majestic animals had become. Winter had been a tough one this year, and I knew they were starving—hence their aggressiveness. They were wolfish skeletons, with their stomachs drawn up tight to their spines, and they were closing in for the kill. Motivated by fear, my trudging pace quickened, and my senses amped-up as I held the axe at port-arms, ready to strike the first one bold enough to come within range. I think they sensed my fear and emitted frenzied howls of excitement. It was a dinner call. But as I neared the truck, they seemed to sense my increased confidence, and they backed off—slightly. Although it wasn't until I yanked hard to open the partially frozen, creaky, diver-side door that they gave one last lonesome howl of defeat, and I was glad to have heard it.

The ol' Dodge didn't disappoint and lived up to its reputation of being "a good starting truck," even with a crappy battery. With my brightest, dim high-beams on, I drove down Moose Pond Road, negotiating frozen ruts and ice flows while relaxing in the solace of not being pursued by hungry predators. This welcome respite from being preyed upon allowed me to contemplate the shock and awe of my latest adventure—*except that I wasn't shocked or awed.* Instead, I was exhilarated. In fact, I felt euphoria—like the lingering excitement you experience when walking out of a theater after watching an action-packed film. By this, I reasoned that I was becoming accustomed to these apocalyptic time-traveling experiences—*or was becoming addicted a better descriptor?*

Saranac Lake was deserted, and it must have been around midnight when I passed the darkened but still open Downtowne Grille. *On a weekday, no less?* I learned a long time ago that when opportunity meets desire, you act, and since I desired a

Leaning Pine, I acted. The bar was empty except for the inattentive bartender and an old guy sitting astride a barstool. This guy looked vaguely familiar, and I sipped my beer and tried to recall where I had met him. This was difficult because all that I could see of his face were ruddy red cheeks framed by long gray hair and an even longer gray beard. Covering most of his head was a brown felt crusher hat bedecked with various trout flies and fishing lures. I noticed in the pocket of his red and black buffalo-plaid shirt was an unlit corn-cob pipe. He dressed as if he had just walked out of the woods. I figured him for a logger or a trapper by his hi-top leather boots and loosely suspender'd Malone trousers. But then it occurred to me, this guy was dressed as an old-time Adirondack guide. That's why he looked so familiar, for I had seen the image of this iconic persona in Adirondack art thousands of times. But no one wore woolies anymore. The new guides had gone high-tech with polypro, fleece, and Gore-Tex. So why was this guy dressed up like this—*did I miss the parade?* Winter Carnival was still going on, and this guy was likely in costume for some event—like the Winter Carnival Parade.

He caught my gaze several times as I tried not to eyeball him, but I couldn't help noticing his flat beer. I figured that he'd been nursing it for a while. In my experience, the Grille usually provides their patrons with plenty of free, salty popcorn—making flat beer an anomaly. *Lousy bartender.*

Catching one too many of my glimpses, the old-timer held my gaze and spoke. "The deer's been work'n' the cedars a fair amount."

This meant that the deer were feeding on cedar, providing bulk but little nutrition—a last resort for starving deer. I responded, "Yep, it's been a long winter."

He said, "Get'n' so cold t'night the thermo-meter might freeze."

I nodded in acknowledgment and was thinking about how easy it was to talk to him when he said, "Mason, I hear'ed thot yer wife's been a'travel'n'."

This was North Country speak for "your wife is having an affair." Even though his tone wasn't malicious or taunting, I was so enraged that I picked up my half-empty glass in preparation to smash it into his face. I got up, hesitated, and then sat my ass back down because I realized that I couldn't hit him. Maybe this was because he was old and had this gentle kindness and wisdom about him, but more than likely it was because I knew he was speaking the truth. That's why I hadn't seen Marlene since my tup off the roof.

I knew this was coming and was an idiot to ignore the signs. Marlene hadn't been madly in love with me since her brief rebellious phase, which I shamelessly took advantage of by marrying her. That was over twenty years ago, but I still look back on that time with fondness.

~*~

I had just started working for the Department of Environmental Conservation as a wildlife technician in Long Island. The job didn't pay much, but it was a starter position for a wildlife biologist, and I was lucky to get it. Most of my classmates were doing volunteer work, or going on for their Ph.D.s (Piled Higher and Deeper) because there were few jobs in the wildlife field. Of course, Long Island is the most expensive place on Earth to live—which is why there was an opening in the Stony Brook office. I think Marlene's father, Reggie, hired a private detective to verify that I was not a ship's master and was instead just a lowly state worker. Upon confirmation of this, he did his best to dissuade Marlene from seeing me—it didn't work. In fact, it had the opposite effect, drawing us even closer, and before I knew it, I was asking Reginald (I wanted to be on his good side for this) for Marlene's hand. This was a big mistake.

I had to listen to a demeaning lecture on our differences in status and how no good would come from our union. As Reggie described, I was merely a brown-collar worker, and Marlene was royalty. I took the "brown-collar" crap to mean that I was a professional outdoorsman, so the insult didn't stick. He further informed me his attorney had drafted a bulletproof prenuptial agreement that would award me nothing upon our probable divorce. Additionally, if I didn't sign it, they would excommunicate Marlene and cut her off from the family's finances. Being an optimist, I took this legal threat as a green light—why else would you have an attorney draft a "prenup" unless you believed the marriage was likely? So we eloped, and I never got around to signing the agreement, but I'm sure my forged and notarized signature is on it. It is surprising what people think they can get away with just because they have the means to out-litigate you.

For a while, after begrudgingly accepting our marriage, Reggie and Darla tried to bring me into the clique. Because social galas are an important part of royal existence, Marlene's parents hosted plenty, and since we didn't live too far from the North Fork, we had to be guests at most. What annoyed the shit out of me when I attended these gala affairs (besides the rarified attitude and hoity-toity mannerisms of the other guests) was that Reggie always introduced me as someone who "works for the government." Actually, what vexed me the most was the *way* he said it, as if "working for the government" implied that I held a critical position within the Department of Defense instead of being an insignificant biologist for the Department of Conservation. I processed this as yet another put-down because of my modest station in life.

This is probably why I spurned his offer of employment for one of his energy companies. Frankly, it was also because if I accepted the job, I would have been working for the "dark side," and I couldn't compromise another of my core values. The position was for an environmental impact statement writer to skirt EPA regulations for oil pipeline projects, and it paid disproportionately well. So being me, I declined his generous offer by telling him it would conflict with my volunteer job as Green Peace commando aboard the SS *Rainbow Warrior.* This bullshit had the desired effect—it enraged Reggie so much that he excommunicated me from the family, and I was so good with it.

As much as I wanted to save the whales, I was actually taking a lateral transfer to upstate New York. The job paid the same, but because of the lower cost of living, moving was like a pay raise. So I was happy, but Marlene was not. Apparently, she had outgrown her rebelliousness and, by our phone bills, I could tell that she had mended fences with her parents. Soon, I was dropping her off and picking her up at the Lake Clear Airport for monthly brainwashing sessions with her parents. I'm fairly certain these meetings had the desired effect because she grew distant. The signs of her dissatisfaction were subtle at first, but when I think back, they were easily recognizable—*because I wanted to see them*. The symptoms were obvious: various out-of-town seminars, the many late nights at work, and the daily love-making dropping off to once a month.

If I had been a grown-up, I would have realized Marlene was young and just missed Mom and Dad, and maybe her girlhood home. Additionally, I would have realized she was working her ass off by starting a real-estate business in the North Country —no easy task. Also, I would have understood this challenging undertaking would involve many late nights and a lot of net-working—not an ideal aphrodisiac. But I couldn't and wouldn't understand because I tend to worry more about what I fear instead of thinking about what I want. Consequently, our hot-blooded relationship became volatile. I realize, now, this was mostly on my part.

I knew Marlene ate a fair amount of shit from parents, relatives, and *former* friends for marrying below her station. She took this in stride, but I resented it, and ironically, I held this against her. I realize I should have seen a shrink for this because I'm still in love with that seasick, auburn-haired, Long Island princess. Instead, I let go of what I wanted. This is why I now feel like I've been hung by my heels and field-dressed.

But, since my real signature wasn't on any pre-martial documents, I had nothing to lose in a divorce court. So I hunkered down and recalled a line out of my old Military Police Field Manual from my army days. I recalled the standard verbiage we used when arresting drunk, disorderly, and fighting soldiers: "THE FIRST ONE TO MAKE A MOVE IS THE FIRST ONE TO GET HURT!" That's right; I wasn't leaving home in a fit of rage or going anywhere. Hopefully, Marlene would be so head-over-heels in love with Freddy (*I figured that's who she was a travel'n' with*) that she'd want to get this thing over with quick. When Marlene got tired of sharing the family homestead with me, she could sign it over, along with my old truck too. Besides, I had more important things to think about than my dysfunctional marriage, like submitting my lesson plans for the summer Adirondack Biology course and ordering materials for the deck job up in Loon Lake.

I found the lesson files on my laptop from last year, printed them, and since I was driving by, mailed them from Santa's Workshop on my way to the Hazelton Sawmill. The envelope would have a Christmasy "North Pole" postmark, which no one would notice. I know this because I used to go out of my way to mail my Christmas Cards from the North Pole, but no one ever commented, so I used this as a shameless excuse to stop sending Christmas Cards. When I got to the sawmill, I spoke to the yardmaster, who informed me that the extra-long cedar planks I needed for the decking weren't available this year. The Hazelton Sawmill only bought from local loggers, and, apparently, this wasn't a good year for cedar. My penchant for "shopping local" had cost me some gas. Therefore, with regret and against my better judgment, I drove to Ray Brook and ordered the decking through Durkis Lumber. After a long process, with the sales associate cursing at his computer while inputting my order, he told me that my cedar would be ready for pickup in about a month and that they would even call me. This would cut it close, but with some long days, I'd have the deck done by Memorial Day.

It was a warm and sunny spring day, but I noticed that the

ground was still frozen, and "mud season" was still a little way off. Up here, mud season is when the snow has melted and the first few inches of the ground thaws, creating a mucky slurry that's about ankle deep. This goop causes many trails to be impassable, and it makes for a messy slog in the woods. But despite the unseasonal, early spring warmth, the forest floor was still snow covered. So on the way home, I just had to drive out of my way and stop at the foundation.

CHAPTER 9

The spirits wasted no time, for as soon as I climbed down the rubble ramp, they plunged me into pitch black. It took a few seconds for my view to adjust to the darkness, but as it did, I realized that the foundation was now a dwelling. The covering I was under was the smoking bird's nest I saw during my last viewing. As I inspected it, I noticed no attempt at thatching of the spruce bows, or any organized form of placement, just random piles of brush with some rotting animal skins thrown over a few spaces. At about the center of this makeshift roof was an area of penetrating sunlight where there was an opening directly over a fire pit with still glowing embers. I reckoned that this opening was their chimney. I also noticed that there was no hinged door or any discernable entrance portal. To enter or exit, the occupants must have pushed the bows aside and rearranged them after. Speaking of the inhabitants, I was glad that the dwelling was unoccupied, for I wasn't yet ready to observe who, or what, lived in this place, but I assumed they were a humanoid species of hunter/gatherers and that's likely what they were away doing. As I looked around, I noticed oblong piles of balsam bows arranged around the fire pit, and I deduced that these were beds. I counted seven. As my point of view moved about the floor, it stopped at a far corner where there was a pile of stinky leaves and scraps of bark. My overwhelmed olfactory sense told me that this was their toilet; at least it was during the night. I reasoned that while no animal wants to foul its nest, making this nocturnal privy was necessary for their survival. Unlike the rare outdoor pleasure that rural males can enjoy during modern times (pissing outside, at night), engaging in this behavior, during this period, would have been hazardous. While the spirits had allowed me to observe the dire wolf/short nose bear spectacle during daylight, I'm sure that these creatures owned the night (along with the sabre-toothed cat), and they did their best hunting then.

I guessed that I must have completed my tour of the dwelling because my view moved outside, beyond the vernal pond (that was still a lake) and down to the riverine valley. The surrounding forest had changed—it was more established with many towering white pine and tamarack trees overhanging the river, although I noted that the jagged peaks of the Stevenson Range were still barren rock. It would be another several thousand years before lichen would get a foothold and break that rock into soil. As I marveled at the maturing woods, I caught a movement in the periphery—and out from the tree line emerged a pack of men.

Actually, it would have been more correct to refer to them as non-primate humans. I knew they weren't Algonquins or Iroquois by their stout build, and by their large, protruding jaws and flat, broad noses. I counted five as they cautiously moved, wary and alert, with quick, jerky advances. But they walked upright, or nearly so, with a slight bend forward, as if tempted to touch the ground with their longish arms. I noticed that they had brown skin, but covered with hair and not fur, and draped over their torso, like a poncho, was an animal skin. Their thick-browed heads were covered from the eyes to the napes of their necks with coarse dark hair, but they exhibited only sparse facial hair. I observed that two members of the pack carried spear-like poles, but they were thick and appeared too heavy to be aerodynamic. Also, the tip of the spear had no blade or flint and was merely whittled to a point. The other members of the pack each carried a wooden club of about three feet long. The pack moved along the riverbank, gradually spreading out, with

73

their eyes cast downward, perhaps looking for animal tracks or edible plants. I was marveling at these earliest of Adirondack hunters when one of them looked up in my direction, as if he could see me.

I thought this to be odd because during all previous viewings I was an invisible spectator, with no form or body —and even the highly developed senses of predatory animals could not detect my presence. But this guy had seen something. *Maybe it was behind me?* And now with his head tilted back, he was sniffing the air as he bared his large wide teeth (with very prominent canines) in a flehmen response, used by predatory mammals to enhance their sense of smell. At this, I attempted to look behind me, and to my surprise, I could. This was remarkable because until this point the spirits had controlled my view. Near as I could tell, there was nothing but dense forest behind me. But as I was surveying my previous path, I heard a vocalization in a series of guttural grunts in front of me. I turned and saw the man was now alerting the pack to my presence—and pointing at me with his club. This was weird because for first time in all of these viewings, I felt self-aware and looked down at myself —what I saw shocked the shit out of me. I had a body—of what species, I could not identify, but it was covered with fur.

Before I had time to examine the spectacle of my new self, I saw that the members of the pack had separated and were rapidly advancing toward me at a dead run. I attempted to talk to them, thinking I could settle them by uttering a sharp command, similar to calming an aggressive dog by yelling "STOP!" But when I attempted to speak, I felt a strange vibrating sensation in my throat, and as my mouth opened, a low-pitched growl ending with a fierce, menacing snarl ensued. I could not speak or even form words. Since my attempt at appeasement had failed, I used my only other viable option, which was to run like hell. Actually, this was more of an instinct than a conscious decision because my body was already moving before I could think to do so. But something was wrong with my hind legs (for some odd reason I thought of them as hind legs); they weren't moving fluidly. As I ran, I looked at them and noticed how stringy-muscled and short they were, and they had this peculiar crooked and gnarled shape—and they bent the wrong way. Also, I was running on the sides of my feet and not on the soles, which would have been far more efficient. During all this self-exploration, I heard the excited vocalizations of the pack as they were rapidly gaining on me. These guys could run, and with their primitive weapons, I had little doubt I would be at a disadvantage if they caught me.

Perhaps it was this dire endangerment that prompted another deep-rooted instinct of my body to kick-in—which was to run on all fours. I found that planting my hands (attached to my incredibly thick and long arms) well in front of me and kicking my hind legs forward and beyond them (like a galloping horse) was the most efficient mode of running. In fact, I was making such good speed that I was leaving the pack behind. Again, I didn't think to do this—my body just did it, and I was damn glad it did.

I moved effortlessly, astounded at the limitless energy and endurance of my form. Even after running (galloping) at full speed for what I estimated to be at least a mile, I was not in the least fatigued and continued to sprint as though I could keep this pace forever. Additionally, this old growth forest was open under the canopy with no brush understory to impede my progress; just a thick blanket of brown needles covered the ground. This made for such easy movement that I was sure of my escape—until I heard rapid footfalls ahead of me. Unfortunately, the lack of obstacles allowed the men to make good progress too. Two spearmen were in front of me and running toward me with points raised. They had driven me into a classic hunter's ambush. I wondered, *Is this the way they hunted the mammoths?* At this, another thought occurred—they weren't chasing me because I was a threat or a danger to them. Instead, I was being hunted because I was their food!

I immediately stopped my advance; I had about fifty feet to the spearmen. It was still too far for a throw of those heavy spears, but they were moving within range quickly. I turned to run back but saw that the clubmen had covered my escape and were closing this gap just as quickly. Since flight hadn't worked, my next instinct was to fight, but something told me that this too would not end well. These guys knew what they were doing and had undoubtedly faced tougher game than me—*whatever the devil I was.* So again, without thought or logic, I let out a thunderous roar as I jumped up and caught a branch—over ten feet above my head! Before I even realized the miracle of what I had done, or became awestruck by my form's agile power, my arms pulled higher and flung me to another tree. And without thought, I repeated this technique of moving through the forest canopy, again and again, each time increasing my distance from the hunters and the likelihood of me becoming their dinner. It surprised me I could move through the trees faster than they on the ground.

What I thought had been a cruel joke of the spirits—which was to give me a body that was several thousand years of evolution behind that of my pursuers—had turned out okay, so far. These guys were good runners, but along the way, they had lost their ability to climb trees, or at least climb trees the way I could. Since I was temporarily out of harm's way, I paused and took stock of my new form. My body was larger and more robust than that of the men, but it had no overt musculature. Frankly, it was as unattractive as it was primitive. Beneath my scraggly fur was a dark and thick skin, which hung and sagged in a most peculiar fashion, as if it couldn't stretch and had to be oversized to allow movement. But this body had tremendous strength and efficiency. I tried to figure out why. *Was it muscle composition, tendon attachment points, or was it just the primordial ferocity of a wild creature?* Since I couldn't see my head or face (nor did I necessarily want to), I felt them with my oversized hands. Near as I could tell, my cranial features were about the same as those of the hunters, with the exception that my face was far hairier. Apparently, I was their ancestor, but they either didn't know or didn't care, and it seemed that they hunted my kind with great contempt. I knew current research supported theories of the convergent evolution of humans. That is, more than one variant of our species coexisted during the same period. But what I didn't realize was that the superseded genus was hunted to extinction by our own kind.

Since I had ceased movement while performing my self-assessment, the hunters had caught up and were now gathered in a group beneath me. I sensed that they were strategizing how to get me on the ground where they had the advantage. Without fear, I had climbed high in the pines seeking to be out of spear throwing range. But now I realized that these guys either hadn't developed this skill or they had never thought to throw a spear. That's why those shafts were so thick. They were mere extended-range, edged weapons, so the men could stab at their prey without being bitten too badly or stomped to death. The guys with the clubs weren't so lucky. If they were driving dangerous prey that turned and challenged them, they had better be good with that stick, or they'd be the dinner. Now that I had time to assess the situation, I realized breaking through the clubmen with my superior strength would not have been difficult. But even so, I was glad to be safe, perched upon a thick pine bow, in my element—the trees.

Just as I was thinking how lucky I was, I heard a loud crack. As so often happens with pines, the branch I was sitting on, without warning, had snapped clean off, right where it had joined the trunk of the massive tree. As I fell, I twisted and flailed, attempting to propel myself toward the only other grabbable branch, which was just above one spearman. I noticed that he was poised with his spear tip up—ready to skewer me if I missed.

~*~

Apparently, I must have missed the limb, because I was standing in knee deep snow, with pine needles in my hair and

Samuel Dean

tree bark in my fingernails. But the hunters were gone, and more importantly, I didn't have a spear sticking out of me.

I probably should have sought post-traumatic stress counseling after that experience, but I didn't. Instead, I returned to the foundation again and again, until the obligations of my present-day life forced me to take a break from this most extraordinary form of tourism. But before my respite, I got to see the moose replace the mammoths as the largest mammal of the Adirondacks. Similarly, the mountain lion supplanted the sabre-toothed cat as the climax feline, and the modern *Canis lupus* superseded the dire wolf as the top canine predator. I observed many generations of beaver, each one a little smaller, until they were reduced to their present size, although they were no less industrious at dam building. Equally surprising was that the fierce, short-nosed bear disappeared altogether, and, over the millennia, the docile black bear roamed the woods, its lesser lumbering form fulfilling the niche of an omnivorous scavenger. The landscape was stabilizing and becoming familiar with that worn "old shoe" look of today's Adirondacks. The colonizing lichen and mosses had created a thin layer of soil on all but the highest of mountains. Consequently, verdant green shrubbery was creeping up those mountains— even to their summits. *Sometimes, I think part of my addiction to these viewings was because of my enhanced vision.*

But during these most recent viewings, I never experienced another atavism or being within a body of any kind. Often, I think one reason I was so fervently drawn to these viewings was to verify that my primitive form had escaped the hunter's spear. I concluded that it (or...I) must have, or I would not have returned to my present self. But despite my persistence during these viewings, I saw no humanoid creatures, non-primate or otherwise. Nor was there evidence of their habitation. Even the foundation's makeshift bird's-nest roof had collapsed and added to its organic floor covering. It appeared to be, as the evolutionists say, "a false start." Humankind had either migrated to or had evolved within this region, only to leave or become extinct within this locale. Whichever they did, they had left no trace, as archeologists have found no evidence of primitive humanoids in the Adirondacks. But I reasoned that this would be consistent with my observations and understandable. I believe this because the primitives made no durable tools. When I was in their dwelling, I noticed that they sharpened some animal bones, like scapulae, as cutting instruments but there were no knives of flint or stone. Even their weaponry was biodegradable, as spears didn't have stone tips and their clubs were mere branches. Their presence, along with any evidence of it, had, like so much of Adirondack history, dissolved into the wilderness.

However, the one thing that wasn't going away was my present obligation to Pug, specifically to finish that damn deck before the sacred start of camping season. It was no surprise that Durkis Lumber hadn't called as they often forgot or just plain didn't bother. This is typical of many Adirondack businesses where the concepts of customer service and follow-up haven't evolved yet. It had been about a month since placing my order, and since I was driving through Ray Brook, I thought I could stop and pick up the decking. I was so wrong. The sales associate, a slack-jawed numbskull, (who seemed more comfortable asking me, "Do you want fries with that?") couldn't find my order. I deduced this wasn't his fault because the previous slack-jawed idiot hadn't placed it. As much as I wanted to dress down this knucklehead, it would not get me the decking I needed in time. I was screwed.

As I was contemplating the value of preventing this kid from spreading his DNA (by choking the shit out of him), I had a thought. *In Bloomingdale, there was a small sawmill that specialized in native woods—just maybe, they'd have what I need?*

I recalled this mill was belt-driven from the power take off of an old Ford 9-N tractor. Whenever a log finished passing through the mill's enormous circular blade, the well-worn tractor engine would backfire three times as it settled back down to its lumpy and uneven idle. There was also a wood-fired kiln for drying lumber, and you could smell when it was in use by its fragrant aroma whenever you were passing through the tiny hamlet of Bloomingdale. However, it must have been a while since I was last here because now a modern, high-speed TimberKing bandsaw had replaced the tractor-driven, circular-saw contraption. Additionally, I didn't smell the kiln because an automated propane wood-drying oven supplanted it. The native Adirondack wood business must be good. I spoke to Rollie, the mill's owner, and he gave me good news and bad news. The good news was that he had more than enough cedar planks for my project. They had been sawed last year and were good and dry. The bad news was that the boards were rough-cut and needed milling before I could use them as decking. Because this was his busy saw'n' season, it would be about three weeks before Rollie could get around to doing this.

Utterly defeated, I trudged through the muddy lumber yard to my truck, where I pawed around until I found my cell phone in the glove compartment. I blew the dust off, turned it on, and to my surprise, it had service. So I called Pug.

Pug informed me that there was, in his words, "No worries," because the camp's owner was on a European canal cruise with her family and would not be opening the camp until the next sacred camping holiday, the Fourth of July. Talk about lousy follow-up and poor communication. Pug had known this when he offered me the job, but it had slipped his mind to mention this little tidbit. I didn't know whether to be pissed or happy. But I ended up choosing the latter emotion when he offered me five hundred bucks for opening the camp after I finished the deck. So I happily trudged back to Rollie and put in my order, who now said it would be about four weeks, which would be about the peak of black fly season. Oh, well, at least I could count on Rollie to mean what he said.

~*~

With little to do for a month except wait for Rollie to mill my boards, I thought about going back to the foundation. And so I did.

Again, upon reaching the foundation's proximal center, I felt that now familiar, peculiar feeling of weightlessness as I observed subtle changes in the landscape. This was so unlike my earliest apocalyptic viewings where I was watching geologic creation. Now that the land forms had stabilized, I had to scrutinize the flora to verify whether I was in the present or the past. More often it was a change of climate that indicated my timeline. But despite my awe at being allowed to witness the past, a disturbing thought gave me pause. That being, I could choose when to travel into the past, for all I had to do was go to the foundation, but I could not choose when to return to the present. This was decided by the spirits or whoever was allowing me these extraordinary experiences. I had almost given up on the bigger question of whether these events were real or the harbinger of a brain tumor.

But, apparently, I hadn't completely given up, because I saved the pine needles and bark from my tree climbing episode. And hoping to prove myself wrong, I contacted my old college buddy, Jim, who worked for Beta Labs in Florida. Jim confirmed that he could carbon date the samples, but since this would be a "government job" (that is, a six-hundred-dollar procedure performed for free as a favor) it would take about a month. Of course, Jim had a crap-load of questions about why I wanted this done, so I made up some bullshit about how I had an Adirondack archeology hobby. I wrapped the samples in aluminum foil and zip-locked them, but hadn't gotten around to mailing them yet.

Nonetheless, I traveled back, and I wasn't thinking about any of this doubtful nonsense as my view moved to the riverine valley. This area, I recognized, was a natural travel corridor for fauna. From here, I had observed the most forms of wildlife, everything from mastodons to non-primate humans. I reasoned that was why my viewpoint was so often brought forth from this perspective—they wanted me to see more than just the trees through this forest.

Without boredom or disappointment, it wasn't long before I noticed a movement along the periphery of the northern side of the forested riverbank. It was human traffic, and there were three of them.

These weren't the forward-leaning primitive hunters I had narrowly escaped; instead, these were lithe, athletic humans, who walked upright and moved in a coordinated manner with one another. I observed that they were no less wary than the early hunters, but their movements weren't the jerky fearfulness of an animal. Instead, they appeared to be scrutinizing and interpreting signs as they moved silently along the riverbank, communicating with hand gestures and soft multi-syllable sounds. They too were hunters, but their methodology had progressed considerably. This revelation caused me great apprehension as I recalled my previous experience of being hunted by humans. I verified I was still an invisible viewing spectator, and I hadn't morphed into a sasquatch or some other form of game.

I recalled reading that there were only two tribes that used the Adirondacks as their hunting ground: the Algonquians and the Iroquois. Neither tribe ever settled up here, but when they met, serious bloodshed ensued as if each were defending their homeland. Now I wished that I had paid attention to Dr. Torrance's lecture on how climate adaptation had influenced the attire of North American tribes. These guys wore chaps made from tanned leather to protect their legs from the puckerbrush. They also had supple leather moccasins laced to their feet. But despite the near freezing temperature, they were barechested, although I noticed a waxy substance smeared thick on their nearly hairless copper-toned skin, and I recalled reading that some tribes rubbed bear fat on bare skin for wind and waterproofing. I guessed that this was an Iroquois hunting party from points south, as the Algonquian tribes from Canada would wear warmer clothing. I marveled at how much humankind had advanced since my last exposure. They now had language and wore clothing made of tanned leather, instead of stinky raw fur. But by far what was most impressive was they were carrying bows.

The development of bow and arrow weaponry was a significant milestone in human advancement. Now a man could take game from a hundred feet, well out of harm's way. Also, they could engage in warfare from a distance, albeit with no less risk, since both factions would likely be similarly armed. Their bows were long, over five feet, and made from small-diameter trees, like ash or hickory. I also noticed they carved the limbs into an oval shape, and tapered them from the handle, so they could bend without breaking. They made their bowstrings from rawhide or sinew. I was trying to observe detail on the construction of their arrows when I realized that I was about to find out—first hand.

For the second time in all of my viewings, I experienced this queer feeling of manifestation and in-fluxing weight. I was trying to sort this out and get a hold of myself when one of the Iroquois looked toward my direction from the trail he was following. This caused me to look down to verify my physical absence, but what I saw shocked me more than the last visage I had inhabited. It was *me*.

Or, at least it appeared to be a younger version of myself with smooth, dark copper skin and long black hair I could feel touching my shoulders. I was naked, and my hair and skin were like that of the hunters, but I had no idea what my facial features were like. However, I must have looked like an Algonquian because these guys wasted no time in stringing their bows and letting a few arrows fly in my direction. But now, I could run fast, using only my legs, and away I ran like a deer, bare-footed, as arrows went zinging past. Hoping to avoid those arrows, I ran through the forest in a zig-zag pattern, always trying to dodge behind big trees and giant boulders. But despite the swiftness of my youthful form, I was no match for three local expert natives, who could also run fast and were armed with bows. Quickly analyzing these facts, I deduced my only chance of survival would be to escape to the present. Unfortunately, this seemed to happen only when I was within the foundation, which was about a mile distant. Although I wasn't sure how this singularity of "going back" occurred, I felt that retreating to familiar terrain was still my best hope.

I had made it to the vernal pool, which luckily had shrunk from a lake back to a pond, when I noticed two unusual paradoxes: one was that the arrows zinging past were less frequent and there was less chatter behind me. This meant the Iroquois had split up and were attempting to flank—probably planning to ambush me on the far side of the pond. I countered by running wide and straight away from the pool, instead of using the animal trail that circumnavigated it. By some intrinsic sense of navigation, I knew exactly where I was going and where my course would bring me to.

The other peculiarity was just straight out strange, and I have no plausible explanation for this phenomenon. But as I ran, I became aware of voices, not from the Iroquois, but from inanimate objects like trees and rocks, and also from wildlife. They were short, brief messages, which were like texts. Only I could hear them, not with my ears, but within my mind. Their voices were subtle and unintelligible at first, but as I became attuned, I heard them with clarity.

For example, as I passed several trees, I unmistakably heard warnings of my foes' advances. *"There is one centurion behind thee, and two are coming from the direction of the wind."*

I jumped over a rock that warned me, *"Be mindful of the venomous serpent that resides in my shadow."*

But as I passed that rock, I heard the rattlesnake say, *"I mean no harm if thee keeps thy distance."*

I also heard the wind that was rushing through the pines proclaim, *"I will bring the rain in three suns."*

It occurred to me that this was why ancient religions worshiped nature and believed everything had a spirit. In this age, humans lived in harmony with the natural world and imagined they could hear the Earth's songs. Sadly, we've lost this ability, *or belief,* as we learned to master our environment.

And I listened to these benevolent spirits with great intensity, for I needed all the assistance with escape and evasion I could get. I remember reading *The Torture Trail of Isaac Jogues* all too well. Father Jogues was a Jesuit missionary who unwillingly became the first white man to see the eastern Adirondacks. I say "unwillingly" because he was captured by, as he wrote, "the Hiroquoise." During the father's forced march through the wilderness, the Iroquois tortured him by beating his body, biting off and crushing his fingers, and burning his arms and legs before ultimately murdering him with an axe. Humans may have progressed since my last encounter, but they still had the savage cruelty of wild beasts within them, and I sure as hell didn't want to find out if this would be my fate.

Instinctively, I cut to the east, and it wasn't long before I saw the depression of the foundation looming. I sprinted and didn't waste time climbing down. I leaped in, landing soft, like an animal. I listened intently but could no longer hear the footfalls of my pursuers, so it seemed my disappearing act had bought me some time. But I knew it wouldn't be long before these expert trackers would find me—and when they did, I'd be trapped!

While I was impatiently waiting, pleading, and crying for my return to the present, I heard the voices' warning: *"You are not safe here. Go forth from this place before it becomes thy grave!"*

Tactically speaking, I knew this was true, but this didn't account for my hope and my best chance of "going back," so I ignored the sage advice. *But how the hell do I make "going back" happen?* Before I could deliberate further, something got my attention—searing pain in my right calf. An arrow had grazed me, and I could see another coming from the same vector. Luckily these were primitive, low-powered bows that were shooting heavy wooden arrows, which were so slow, I could see them coming. With my catlike reflexes, I easily ducked them—glad that compound bows and carbon fiber arrows hadn't been invented! Without regard, the other two Iroquois were reaching the foundation, (which I now thought of as a death pit), and I knew I wouldn't be able to dodge the arrows of all three archers. *What to do?*

With death a certainty, I was thinking about making the timeless gesture of surrendering by raising my hands, merely to delay this outcome, when I heard, *"Use me as thy shield."*

I looked toward the voice and saw a slice of flat rock that had exfoliated from a boulder. It was an oval, about two by three feet, and approximately an inch thick—a perfect shield! The slab must have weighed over fifty pounds, but to my adrenaline-charged young muscles, it seemed weightless as I grabbed it. And as soon as I moved it, I saw my old weathered white hands poking out of my jacket sleeves, and they were holding this incredibly heavy stone. I had returned!

CHAPTER 10

I didn't know it then, but I had discovered something critically important. But before I could get the concept, a large dark shadow enveloped me. As I rapidly became aware of my surroundings, I looked up at the rim of the foundation and saw the source of the shadow. It was a mature black bear, likely a sow, a female. I always feel lucky when I'm able to see one of these docile creatures, but she was snapping her jaws, appearing agitated and aggressive toward me. But I still wasn't concerned because black bears rarely attack unless you come between a sow and her cubs. Just as I had finished that thought, I heard a loud bawling behind me. Shit! I had known the source before I turned to look—two of her cubs had climbed into the foundation, probably to investigate the strange smelling catatonic creature within. Apparently, when I showed signs of life, the frightened cubs retreated to the foundation's back wall. I was stuck. The angry sow was pacing the rim in front of me and the cubs were blocking my retreat. Complicating the situation was that the easiest point of exit, the rubble stone ramp, was also in front of me. The sow looked as if she would climb down and give me a thrashing at any moment, and I knew if I made the slightest movement toward her cubs, she would launch. So I moved in the only direction available—up. There was a large, curly-bark birch tree beside me that I figured was climbable, especially in my amped-up state, so up I went. After shinning up about ten feet, and hanging on for what seemed like an hour, the sow calmed down and entered the foundation, gathered her cubs, led them up the ramp, and beat feet.

I was so glad to climb down, as my arms were aching and were about to give out, but what really hurt was my right calf. Once on the ground, I gave it a look and saw it was bleeding from a lateral incision. I also noticed a feather embedded in the wound!

Since this wasn't a mortal wound, albeit a painful one, I waited until I got home before extracting the feather and patching up. The long and straight feather appeared to be from a bird of prey, like a hawk, hence its use as an arrow fletching. With that revelation, I rinsed it with distilled water, bagged it, and since I hadn't sent my other artifacts to Jim for carbon dating, I added this one to them.

Deep within, I knew this was useless. I really didn't believe I was time traveling or being chased by Indians, or Neanderthals, I was merely experiencing some sort of transcendental dreaming. *But why it occurred only at the foundation was the real mystery.* I could even explain my souvenirs of lacerations, feathers, bark, and pine needles—they were just the aftereffects of active sleepwalking. Even so, I needed to prove to myself that I was merely reliving college history lessons I had slept through.

And that was what I believed—right until Jim sent me the results.

~*~

Black fly season isn't so bad if you're a local—it's just annoying. Although, I must admit, I shamelessly exaggerate the horrors of this season to people I don't like and don't want moving up here. That's why they call black flies the saviors of the Adirondacks. To tell the truth, they *are* a monumental pain in the ass, especially if you're trying to build a deck through clouds of the little demons. And this season they were so thick I could only see clearly in the wake of my hammer swings. I know I could use bug dope like DEET, which works the best, but it also makes my drill handle sticky because it melts plastic. Natural concoctions like cedar and gardenia oil work for a short while, but you spend more time re-applying them than doing anything else. Plus, the combination makes you smell like a flowery telephone pole for weeks. The old timers would work through the black fly season by maintaining a constant smudge fire or by smoking a noxious cigar. Either way, it was more smoke than I wanted to breathe, so I tolerated them as best as possible. But as soon as both of my hands were tied up doing something critical, one would fly into my nose while another into one of my ears; after buzzing around inside my noggin they'd swap places and fly back out. Despite these unwelcome cranial intrusions, usually only my wrists suffered nearly painless bites, but boy did they itch for days.

That's pretty much the same for everyone—a lot of itch from a few bites and plenty of cocktail conversations to last the year. Except, there was this one guy who nearly bought the farm.

The story goes that a man from New York City came up for one of those guided spring bear hunts that these private hunting clubs sponsor. Supposedly these hunts are legal under the auspices of a private game preserve license. But really, I think this is bullshit, with these clubs providing bear hunting over bait and all. But anyway, the city guy gets dropped off at his baited tree stand in the twilight of early morning.

Before leaving, his guide asks if he has bug dope and a head net, to which city guy says, "No need for such toxins or annoyances, for I've been bathing in distilled water, and taking large doses of vitamin B-12 for weeks. I am invisible to insects!"

The guide says, "Okay, then. I'll be back to pick you up at noon. Good luck."

The guide dutifully comes back at noon, but his client is missing. So the guide, being a good tracker, follows his trail. A few yards from the stand, he finds the guy's rifle on the ground. The guide also follows his tracks in and out of an icy pond. Short ways away the guide sees an area of disturbed dirt. So he digs, and low and behold he finds his client all bitten up and in shock from millions of black fly bites. Once the sun came up, the poor guy discovered that an Adirondack black fly doesn't care how clean you are, or what vitamins you take. The bloodthirsty demons drove the man so crazy he jumped into the pond, and when that didn't work, he buried himself.

Now the deer flies, whose season peaks in July, are the opposite. Unlike the painless but itchy black fly bites, deer fly bites hurt like hell but there are no lingering aftereffects. Also, deer flies are easy to manage because they instinctively prey on hairy things, like deer. So all one needs to do is to wear a hat and the frustrated flies will harmlessly buzz you, smelling the meal but not knowing where to bite, even if you're not wearing a shirt. Either way, the dragonflies gobble-up both the black and deer fly pests by late July. This is probably why Adirondack folk worship dragonflies.

Without regard, I'd have to embrace the suck because I made the commitment to get this deck done and have the camp opened by the Independence holiday weekend, even if it meant working through the peak of the fly season. So verily I toiled, swatting and cursing until, at last, I did it.

~*~

Next in the queue was the Adirondack Biology course. I knew this was likely to be my last one as the college board was giving me the redheaded stepchild treatment. To be honest, I didn't give a damn. After all, I'd stolen the course from Dr. Torrance, so it only fitted that the college should steal it from me and give a job to a real professor. Besides, I was getting too old for two weeks of wilderness camping. Tents are for kids.

Speaking of kids, they were the one thing I would miss, especially the students of this last class. Unlike my previous classes, where they couldn't wait for my bedtimes, these students would actually beg for my fireside lessons. They reminded me of children trying to avoid bedtime by asking for just one more story. It surprised me that this class seemed truly enthralled by my *first-hand* renditions of Adirondack history. I even tried torturing them with tales of geological formation, but to no avail, they would ask for even more. At first, I thought that it was some new variant of marijuana that made anything seem more interesting to them, but I noticed that they would consistently wait until the fire nearly died before breaking out the dope. One student mentioned that this made it more difficult for the rangers to bust them.

Of course, they'd politely offer old Professor Brocke to imbibe, but when I smelled burning rope, it was my chance to end the session and escape to my tent for a rye nightcap. But even so, with almost two hours of fireside history lessons every night, I ran out of material before that course ended. I never imagined that would happen. What's with these kids today?

CHAPTER 11

With my only two paying jobs over for the summer, I looked for another job. I expected that I would soon hear from Marlene's attorney, and knew when I did, my response would cost me some money. I wanted to discuss this with Marlene first, but I couldn't find her. I needed to talk to her because I was in better shape and in a better frame of mind than when she had abandoned me. It was not lost on me that as my everyday vision improved my anger waned. I saw in color now, almost as bright as in my viewings. I also experienced mixed feelings of forgiveness and penitence. I was fairly sure we could have worked this out, but then...this happened.

It had been an unusually dry spring, and the summer was even drier; consequently, a lot of shallow wells kicked. So I got a part-time job delivering bulk water for Rudeau's Sand and Gravel. They had this unbelievably deep artesian spring in their mine that was overflowing with pure North Country water. From this spring I'd fill the thousand-gallon tank that was strapped to the bed of one of their old army surplus flatbed trucks and deliver water to their customers. Since they do not anticipate dry wells in the Adirondacks, a lot of folks had no provisions to store bulk water, but they had to pay for the whole load whether or not they used it all. So typically they'd have me fill a few of those fifty-gallon, blue plastic barrels, several of those ubiquitous five-gallon pails, and every pot, kettle, and vessel in the house that could hold water. Since this hardly made a dent in my thousand-gallon tank, in desperation, many folks would have me dump the rest in their well. This act, I knew, was useless, unless you consider replenishing the deep, subterranean aquifer that their pumps can't reach useful. Often, even after overfilling their wells, I'd still be returning to the pit with a couple hundred gallons or more.

And so it was one time when returning with a sloshing, half-empty load that I drove past this beautiful chalet that was over-looking the High Peaks on the Loj Road. I stopped the truck just past the driveway because, with my keen hunter's eye, I simultaneously noticed several interesting things about the quaint residence:

It was for sale. The sign boasted "Exclusive Listing" and Marlene's name.

The property was a seasonal ski chalet, and since it was off-season, its owners weren't around.

Marlene's luxury SUV was parked, somewhat furtively, under the balcony that doubled as a carport.

Frederick's BMW was wedged, tightly, bumper to bumper, next to Marlene's SUV.

Of course, I thought, *how fornicatingly appropriate.*

I had long suspected *(and warned)* that these two were *canoodling!* But now I had proof, and although I wasn't surprised to verify this, it surprised me at how angry it made me. Today was one of those hot, sultry summer days, and I noticed that Freddy had left the Beemer's sunroof open a crack to vent the heat. Perfect!

In a not-so-well-thought-out act of revenge, I backed the old army truck within hose range of Freddy's rig and filled its interior with crystal-clear water through the sunroof opening. It surprised me, the watertight integrity of this vehicle. There was not a drip from the doors or windows–that's German engineering for you. It also surprised me at how much water the interior of the SUV held, as my truck's tank was nearly empty by the time the water level crested the sunroof. I think BMW should use this feature in their advertisements. And since fornicating Freddy was so meticulously clean, there was no flotsam nor any telltale signs I had filled his car with water, save for the bulging tires and compressed suspension. Boy was he going to be surprised when he opened his door.

My childish act of vandalism did little to assuage my feelings because the event still enraged me as I drove the empty truck back to the pit to get refilled for my next delivery.

~*~

After the last delivery, I realized that in my current mental state, I needed an escape. So my top choices were the Downtowne Grille or the foundation. I decided to do both, and since the foundation was on the way home, it would be first.

It didn't take long for my vision to begin. As soon as I entered the pit, the rocks began to shed moss and rearrange. One by one, more huge boulders rolled into the pit and stacked along the perimeter, making it an actual foundation. *But who or what was doing this?* Soon the stone walls became plumb, and the scene darkened as a roof formed overhead. I noticed that above-grade walls of stacked logs supported this roof. These walls were only about two feet high, but this architecture represented a significant advancement in engineering over the last inhabitants of the foundation. The dirt floor of the pit was still the living level, but the log walls provided headspace and some light from several opaque window apertures. These appeared to be covered with cloth or greased paper, which allowed bright sunlight to penetrate. Even the roof seemed to have been constructed in an ordered fashion with log rafters and bark strips arranged as singles. However, the cabin's door consisted of only a blanket, and I also observed that there was still no chimney—just a hole in the bark roof over the corner fire pit. I also noticed the adjacent rock walls were blackened and the logs above the fire pit were charred. Not exactly code; no wonder there were so many fires in those days.

As my view moved about, I noticed a flickering illumination emanating from the corner opposite the fire pit. It was coming from what the old timers used to call a slush lamp. I've read that slush lamps were necessary, not only for light but also as a source of flame to keep the fire going, since matches weren't invented until the early 1800s. These lamps typically consisted of a tin of animal fat, with some sort of wicking material. This one had a pine knot for a wick, and it also smelled bad enough to be burning some kind of putrefied flesh. But more interesting than the slush lamp was the shelf it was sitting on—for it was the stone slab that I had attempted to use as an arrow shield during my last escapade. Only now the slab was neatly set into the foundation's corner and tightly cantilevered between two cornerstones; thus it was a permanent part of the structure. It then dawned on me—this is that recurring thought I kept trying to clarify. Since the stone slab was to become an important part of the foundation, I wasn't allowed to mess with it. I could interact with the past but couldn't change it. *This rule would be important to remember the next time I needed to make my escape to the present.*

Other than the lamp, there was no human presence at or around the cabin. But by the smell of skins, rotting bait, and scent lures, I deduced that the foundation was now serving as a trapper's seasonal cabin, and its resident was out checking the trap line. Having seen enough, I decided to test my theory. I grabbed hold of the stone slab shelf and gave it a shake. Sure enough, it worked. I found myself back in the present, with my hands on the stone slab, which was now lying on the leaf-covered ground. This was fantastic! I had finally discovered a means of control over these dreams, or flights of fancy—or whatever the devil they were.

~*~

The hike out of the woods had significantly sharpened my thirst, so my next stop had to be the Grille.

Again, it amazed me the place was empty, but then again, it

was a Tuesday afternoon. The only occupant was the old-time guide who was sitting at the bar, nursing a beer. I kept eyeballing him as I downed my second Leaning Pine. I didn't mean to be rude, but since I had recently witnessed the proof of his last prophecy, I kept expecting him to say, "I told ya so." But he didn't.

Instead, just as I had finished my last gulp, I heard him say, "Ya know them state boys is gett'n' a warrant for ye, after whatcha done to that feller's car."

At first, I didn't think he was talking to me, as he never looked up from the glass of amber liquid in front of him. I looked around behind me to see if he was having a conversation with an unseen accomplice but saw no one. It then occurred to me that I should ask him how in the hell he knew what I had done to Freddy's Beemer.

But when I turned back toward him to ask, he was gone. Weird.

On my way home, I picked up the mail. Among the bills, Ace Hardware coupons, and donation requests was a manila envelope with Jim's return address.

~*~

I was still semi-lucid after guzzling two high-alcohol Leaning Pines on an empty stomach (this means I was half drunk), but my curiosity triumphed over slumber. At the kitchen table, I tore open Jim's letter with the grace of a five-year-old unwrapping a Christmas present. I thought the first page of the report was merely a bunch of boilerplate disclaimers about carbon dating error factors because of isotopic variation. That was until I came to a long explanation about the difficulty in dating the submitted samples due to the difficulty in defining the boundary of the beginning of the current *Holocene epoch* and the end of the *Pleistocene epoch*. What... *why the hell were they explaining this?*

The second page listed the samples and their estimated age

range, in years, Before Present:

SAMPLE	RADIO CARBON AGE (BP)	CALIBRATED AGE (BP)
Pinus strobus (Eastern White Pine)		
Bark and Fascicles	**18,000-29,000**	**11,400-14,900**
Accipitor gentiles (Forest Raptor – extinct)		
Scale (feather)	**1,450-1,700**	**1,150-1,350**

Holy Shit!

Attributing my interpretation to my inebriation, I calculated that I probably should go to bed, because this was contrary to everything that I believed, and to what I had expected. After cleaning up, I went into the bedroom with my head still spinning, but as I pulled back the Hudson Bay Blanket, I got it. Jim was just messing with me!

~*~

I didn't sleep well and woke up with a headache, so I swallowed a couple of aspirin with my coffee. It was too early to call Jim, but I thought I should give Marybeth a call before heading to work at Rudeau's, just in case the old guy was right. Marybeth described herself as just the "dumb dispatcher," but in truth, she ran the business, and there wasn't any aspect of it, or local politics, that she didn't know. If there was a warrant out for me, she'd know, even before the judge signed it.

Marybeth: "Rudeau's."

Me: "Hey, how's my good-look'n' girl today!"

Marybeth: "Mason, whatcha done! There was a couple a

troopers ask'n' for ya, just now. They said thot you flooded some feller's car yesterday with our water truck!"

Me: "That's nonsense. On the way back to the pit from my last delivery, I noticed that the truck had a low tire, so I dumped the leftover until I could get air at Central Garage. There wasn't any car within fifty feet of that discharge."

Marybeth: "Well, them purple ties tol me a different story, an I think they're com'n' to talk to ya. I told them thot I didn't have your address on file ona conna that you was a temp. That slowed 'em, but you know they got it by now, and it's a wonder you ain't in jail already!"

Me: "Thanks, Marybeth—you're my girl! And I think I'm a gonna be sick today."

Holy She-ite!

It is an old army habit of mine to always have a go-bag ready, and I did. But it was only stocked with clothing and emergency gear, and I needed food, so I dumped the refrigerator into a cooler and threw it into the back of the truck. I also left the cabin's door unlocked, just like I did every morning that I intended to return. This would tie up the trooper warrant squad by tricking them into staking out my cabin instead of looking for where I really was—which was going to be Earl's old hunt'n' camp.

Earl had built his camp way off-road and ironically on Camp Road "E." It was also conveniently within hiking distance to the foundation, where I reckoned I'd be idling away even more of my time. Earl was getting up in years and hadn't used his camp in quite a while. Several times a year, I would offer to bring him there, but he always declined. However, being a generous man, he allowed me to use it, but I never dreamed that I'd be using Earl's camp to lam from the law.

This camp has a sheltered structure, but to call it a cabin is really a stretch. It's more like an enclosed lean-to, but from the outside, it looks exactly like a pile of construction and demolition debris. However, it has a functional HVAC system in the form of an antique pot-bellied woodstove. It also has running water—that is, only if you run to the creek and get it. But, Earl's hunt 'n' camp was as far off the grid as it was away from any paved road. For me, in my current self-inflicted, jacked-up situation—it was perfect!

~*~

And so it was.

I found myself burning more daylight at the foundation, but I didn't always "go back." Most often, I would sit for hours, just contemplating my situation and my place in the cosmos. *I think they call this meditating?* Whatever it was, it was relaxing. After many a diurnal experience, whether viewing the present or the past, I'd hike back to Earl's cabin at twilight, just in time to start a fire, cook a can of beans, and down a couple of beers. After using the outhouse, I would climb into one of the cabin's rustic bunks and sleep soundly, with the womblike feeling that one gets from being surrounded by towering pines and serenaded by the calls of barred owls and the lonesome howls of the coywolves. My morning alarm clock was the cacophony of bird songs and the incessant hammering of woodpeckers. After perking a pot of coffee over the fire, I'd sit on the porch with a cup and listen to the world continue to wake up. I may have been roughing it, but my escapism was heaven.

During my meditations I had several brief viewings and watched many improvements to the virtual world of the foundation. For example, it now sported a cabin that had grown to a full story, with log walls and a floor of roughhewn planks. Thus, the foundation had become a cellar. The cabin even had a real door, and a stone fireplace complete with a chimney along its northern wall. I realized that one day, in the distant future, this chimney would collapse to become the rubble ramp I used for access.

I say my infrequent viewings were brief, but the time spent

in the past was significant. This was not unlike a dream where one can experience days of adventure during mere seconds of slumber. It was during one of these interludes when again I felt the weird and weighty pull of gravity upon my viewpoint. I realized that I was assuming another form, and luckily not that of an animal or an Indian. Instead, it was that of a young boy. I deduced that the child was pre-pubescent and estimated his age to be about ten years. Actually, I knew this, but this young body belied its age, as it was not soft, as you would expect of a present-day ten-year-old. In fact, this body was scarred, hard, and sinewy—apparently forged and beat-up from the hard labor of wilderness living. As I melded into his form, I felt myself come alive with resilience and youthful agility, but something told me that this would not be a happy childhood.

Intrinsically, just as I had known my age, I knew my history, as if a database had been uploaded into my brain. I learned that I lived with my father, a capable but very ornery man. I realized that this was the wood-gathering man I had seen during one of my earliest viewings. His disagreeable personality may have been from the pain of the ball that was still lodged in his pelvis from a war wound. *But from what war—the Civil War?* Or was his constant anger the result of being paid for his service in untillable Adirondack land? I understood that he was a farmer at heart, but since this proved impossible, he had become a fur trapper and a maple sap distiller—ventures that he knew little of when he migrated here. I also learned that before any of my siblings could be conceived, my mother had died of "consumption," *or was it the vapors, which was really tuberculosis?* This too may have contributed to my father's ill-temperament, for a man without the help of a homemaking wife and the free labor from a slew of children was at a disadvantage in this wild country. Added to this was the likelihood he hadn't gotten laid since my mother died. I observed that he buried her by the vernal pond with only a crude cross, made from sticks, with not even an inscription marking her grave.

As I walked toward the pond, I observed several axe heads suspended by ash tree saplings growing out of their eyes. At first, I was bewildered by the scene, but then I realized that this is how they replaced broken handles—they grew them! The result was an axe handle that would never come off and be far more durable than anything you could buy at a hardware store. The only problem was that the process of replacing a broken handle would take ten to fifteen years! People were patient during this period, but they had to be because hardware stores weren't in existence yet. Time seemed to be limitless during this age.

I was examining one of the double-bit axe heads by rotating it to see if the sapling had formed an oval shape to fit its eye— when the next thing I felt was a sharp, knee-buckling blow on the top of my head! As I recovered consciousness, and found myself on the ground, I saw my father standing over me.

My first thought was a tree limb had fallen on my head, and he had come to my aid, but then he issued a stern reprimand. "FOOL—DINNA TOUCH 'EM, LEST THEY GROW CROOKED!"

At this, I realized that it was he who had cracked me on the head! Although my brain was addled, I remember being amazed at how silently he could walk through the woods, even with his switch hip. I never touched those axe heads again.

I had many chores, chief among them were fleshing pelts and splitting wood. Luckily I was no stranger to either task. During my fieldwork I had gutted and skinned many a fur-bearer at the initiation of a necropsy, and splitting wood was a regular part of North Country life—even during the present time. As directed, I chopped and stacked cords of wood alongside the cabin until nightfall, but the last armful went into the cabin for the evening fire. I learned that keeping the fire going dissuaded mosquitos and other flying pests from entering the cabin through the many chinks in the chinking. It was a good thing that the drafty fireplace didn't put out much heat because my sleeping quarters were in the loft right above it.

One evening I had split a particularly large load of firewood and needed both arms to carry it into the cabin. So I stuck the axe in the chopping block and left it there while I took the load into the cabin. I was stacking the wood by the fireplace when again blinding pain befell me on the top of my head.

This time I realized that a stone hadn't dropped from the mantle, it was just my father's way of reinforcing his reprimand. "BRING THE AXE IN, OR THE GOL-DAMN INJUNS A'STEAL IT!"

What the hell was with hitting kids on the head? No wonder there were so many idiots during this time, for their brains had been injured during childhood. But this knock on my noggin brought back my memory of the first vision of my father at the cabin *Now I had the answer to why he took the axe inside.*

And I never left it outside, at night, again.

~*~

One morning, my father was in an unusually good mood. He told me we were making a trip into town and to hitch the horse to the wagon. While I had never done this, it wasn't too hard to figure out—just connect every strap to a buckle and make sure that most of them go around the horse. We had one horse and two oxen. The powerful but slow moving oxen were presently used for dragging logs and pulling stumps, but they were originally brought up here for plowing, an endeavor that had not occurred for some time. The flatbed wagon had these oversized, five-foot-diameter, solid wooden wheels for negotiating rough terrain; but since Father had told me to hitch the horse, I reasoned that we would travel on a road. Before we left, he told me to load the wagon with five raw (unfleshed) beaver pelts, a jug of maple syrup, and a shovel. From this, I inferred that we were going to a store to do what my father called "some trad'n'." *But why were we taking the shovel?* I couldn't have been more wrong about traveling on a road, or about going to a store.

We made a harrowing passage up this mountain trail to some hovel in the forest, a place that my father called Spike Brown's cabin. Several times I was certain we would lose both horse and wagon by pitching off the many cliffs and steep slopes that the narrow trail traversed. But my father appeared unphased by the danger, and I stayed at the reins because I feared getting smote on the head more than falling down the mountain.

When we got to Spike's cabin, we found him sitting on a stump, whittling a black cherry gall into a bowl. Spike was a big man, but his long gray beard and bent frame told me he was not young and probably not long for living up on this mountain. *But where would he go?* There were no old folks' homes or eldercare institutions yet. Spike also had this strange, raw-appearing scar patch on one side of his bald head—like it had been burned or melted in a fire. On the way down the mountain, I risked a crack to my head by asking Father about the scar and was informed that years ago, an "Injun" had tried to scalp Spike while he was sleeping. The task wasn't completed because Spike had served as one of Roger's Rangers (our army's first special forces unit) and always slept with a big knife under his pillow. By watching him convert the gnarled gall into an attractive bowl, I could tell, even in his state of declination, that he was still skilled with a knife.

While I sat on the wagon, my father talked to Spike and shared with him the dregs of a bottle that I guessed was whiskey. There was a fair amount of settlement in the tobacco-juice-colored liquid, and I wondered if its sought-after effects were the result of toxicity. They soon shook hands, and Father told me to get the shovel and showed me where to dig.

By the ease of digging and the size of the plot of disturbed earth, I realized that I was uncovering a fresh grave, and I dreaded what I would find. But it relieved me when my shovel hit matted gray fur and exposed the body of a mature timber wolf. It was a large specimen, and by its lack of rigor and slipping fur, I estimated that it had been dead for at least three days. With great exertion, I dragged the dead weight of the wolf to the wagon. Without effort, my father heaved the heavy, stinky carcass aboard, and gave Spike the pelts, the syrup, and another partial bottle of turbid whisky from his knapsack.

I was absolutely perplexed why we were trading such valuable commodities for the dead and rotting wolf remains. I was further flabbergasted when, at the precipice of a cliff, Father stopped the wagon, and with his knife, removed the wolf's head and then pitched the body off the cliff! *What the heck was going on—had he drank too much of that bad whisky?*

We proceeded over a rutty trail that paralleled the Saranac River to a small settlement I recognized as Bloomingdale, only I don't think it was officially named yet. The tiny hamlet merely consisted of a collection of small cabins sprawled around a sawmill. The mill was water-powered by a river that one day would be named Sumner Brook, but presently it was called Negro Creek. Within this hovel of ramshackle structures was a saloon called Gruffy's Tavern, and by the trodden dirt path to it, I surmised that this establishment saw a fair amount of use. I wasn't sure why, but thought it was fortunate that it was closed this morning. But there was a big man sitting on the worn treads of the tavern's wobbly stairs. The man dressed much the same as my father, and his name was Charlie. Charlie had fought in the war alongside Father but had taken his land grant in Bloomingdale, where he settled to work at the mill. I observed that he was missing the thumb of his right hand and two fingers of his left hand. I realized that this was the toll of a present-day sawmill worker as there was no OSHA yet and safe working conditions weren't the mill owner's priority.

Like Spike Brown, Charlie was a big man, but he appeared undernourished. He must have been near the same age as my father but appeared many years older, with an ashen skin color and much sagging flesh hanging off his bones. Also, grooming wasn't his priority, as it had been awhile since his unkempt salt and pepper beard and dull hair had seen scissors or comb. And both his skin and hair had lost their vigor long ago. *Perhaps he was living with an undiagnosed cancer?* Aside from his haggard physical appearance, Charlie had a lively personality, and this morning, like my father, he seemed to be in a particularly good mood. Charlie climbed aboard our wagon and sat in front, on the buckboard with Father, as I kept the smelly wolf's head company in the bed. We traveled north along a decent trail that paralleled Sumner Brook, which I recognized was the future State Route 3. As we proceeded, Father and Charlie spoke in low tones, like they were strategizing, while I tried not to puke and pondered why we were transporting this stinky wolf's head for so long.

It was about an hour after noon when we got to a two-story building sited along the trail where the brook crossed. By its crude hand-painted sign, I saw that it was the Franklin Town Hall. It then became clear that Father was going to redeem this wolf for a bounty. In accord with these times, municipalities paid bounties on these predators to eradicate them for the protection of domestic livestock. *But why did he pass the nearby St. Armand Town Hall, which was right in Bloomingdale? And why did he need Charlie's help, because it was my assigned job to portage this stinky wolf head?*

But, like so many other mysteries of the North, all this would soon become abundantly clear.

As expected, Father told me to grab the wolf's head and follow him into the building. Charlie stayed with the wagon and made an elaborate show of hitching the horse to a cedar post erected specifically for this purpose. Carrying the head with my arms fully extended, I followed Father up the rickety stairs to an office on the second floor of the Town Hall. The door was half-open, and as Father knocked, I heard a familiar voice say, "C'mon en." *Holy shit, it was him!*

The old Adirondack guide was sitting behind a desk, only now he was outfitted as the town clerk. He dressed in a well-worn, rumpled, dark gray suit with raw leather patches that were roughly stitched to the elbows. But his flowing white hair and long beard were exactly as I recalled from when I had seen him at the Grille—I swear that it was him, which made little sense. But again, I recognized his familiar voice when he directed me to set the head on the sill of an open window. As I did this, the clerk (or, should I call him the guide?) asked Father a series of questions like his name, address, and where he had shot the wolf. And with a black quill pen made from a raven's wing feather, he scribbled the data on a yellowed page of a large, dog-eared ledger. The clerk then retrieved a skeleton key from the top desk drawer and walked over to a huge floor safe. Without difficulty, he unlocked this over-sized and very rusty ironclad lock that secured a logging chain, wrapped several times around the safe. He returned with a wad of sawbucks (ten-dollar bills), and with the speed and dexterity of a card shuffler, counted out six and gave them to my father. The clerk returned the rest of the bills to the safe, but I noticed that the door remained unlocked. He further directed that Father needed to "make his mark in the ledger" next to his name. At this, I realized that my father could not read nor write, as the clerk had to guide his pen hand to the place on the page. While Father was occupied, the clerk withdrew a gnarled walking stick that was leaning alongside his desk and pushed the wolf's head out of the window. As he replaced the stick, I swear that I saw him wink at me. Father returned the drippy quill to the clerk and thanked him. Thinking we were done, I was about to leave when I heard footfalls on the stairs. It was old Charlie, and he was carrying the wolf head!

Again the clerk asked the same questions of Charlie and entered his answers in the ledger. Only this time, after paying Charlie another six sawbucks, the clerk withdrew a straight razor from his pocket and cleanly cut the ears from the head. He placed the ears in a still smoldering pot-bellied woodstove and soon an unbelievable stench of burning hair and rotten flesh filled the room. I heard the clerk quietly remark that "this wolf has killed enough green sheep."

While choking back a gag, Charlie said thanks and headed down the stairs. Father again thanked the clerk as he peeled off a sawbuck and left it on his desk. As I turned to exit the office, I heard the clerk say, "Be mindful and keep a close watch on yourself, Mason. These are difficult times."

At the wagon, I saw Charlie give Father four of his sawbucks, which meant that old Charlie had earned twenty dollars for his limited participation in this scheme. More significantly, my father netted ninety bucks, minus the maple syrup and whiskey he traded with Spike Brown for the carcass.

While I wasn't entirely sure, I thought this was like a year's worth of wages during this day. No wonder why my father was in such a good mood. This also answered my question of why we traveled all the way to Franklin for the bounty—they paid well! *But if they needed to cull the wolf packs, why did we have to buy one?*

~*~

Unlike when we picked Charlie up, now the scene at Gruffy's Tavern was lively and chaotic. Along with much yelling and cursing from within the tavern, there were scores of horses and oxen in various stages of health, hitched to the posts in front of the rickety stairs of the establishment's entrance. There was even an adult black bear chained to a tree. Fortunately for the horses, it was a short chain. The bear was methodically pacing, dragging the heavy chain its entire length of about ten feet before reversing direction. I heard riotous laughter and glass breaking from within the tavern. To my surprise, Father hitched our horse to a post as Charlie headed up the stairs with a vigor that defied his appearance. I did not think this was a good idea and foolishly risked a crack on the head by stating so. But, luckily, *or unluckily*, Father was so happily distracted by the tempestuous raging within the tavern he paid no attention to my warning. As I reluctantly followed him in, a shot rang out, and then another two. In the near distance, I heard more glass breaking and some men cheering. It appeared to be random gunfire or target shooting. *But what were they shooting at?*

Undaunted and seemingly unaware of the rowdy ambiance, Father walked straight to the bar and ordered a whiskey. The barkeep, an unruly, vile-looking man who, like most of the patrons, had not seen a bar of soap or even a good rain shower in some time, placed a nearly full bottle of turbid amber liquid in front of my father. Alongside this unlabeled bottle, he also set a short glass that was so hazed from years of use, it appeared opaque. I noticed a rough-sawn plank hanging above the bar. The primitive, hand-painted inscription on it stated: WHISKEY —A DOLLAR A GLASS. I thought this was not good, as Father was flush with cash, and except for the few swigs while tradin' with Spike, he had not tasted the nectar (as he called it) in some time. I spied Charlie through the line of scrappy trappers and quarrelsome lumberjacks at the bar. He was sitting alone with a similar setup of a whiskey bottle and dirty glass. Again, this was not good, as I was stuck in a kid's body and couldn't do much to rescue two inebriated men.

I was so thirsty and pretty sure this place didn't have an issue with serving underage kids because that law hadn't even been considered yet. So in my most manly, prepubescent voice, I asked the barkeep for a beer and was subsequently informed that they don't have beer. At this, I looked around and noticed that the only beverage this tavern served was whiskey, in those ubiquitous unlabeled brown bottles. Although the barkeep offered me the standard fare of bottle and glass, I declined, knowing that I would need to keep my wits keen, for both Father and myself.

Tough-looking men packed the smoke-filled bar, most of them wearing a long-barreled pistol in a holster. Those who did not sport a firearm had a big sheathed knife on their belt. There was also a gun rack in the corner filled with Winchesters, Remingtons, and the various long guns of the patrons. At a sturdy table made from thick, hand-hewn planks, two lumberjacks were arm wrestling. Aside from their brawny physiques, I could tell that timber was their profession because of the axes stuck in their belts. On the table, at the landing spot for either would-be loser's hand, was a broken shot glass with its razor-sharp shards pointed up. I realized this was to confirm the loser of the contest by gushing blood. Despite the din, I heard the metallic double-click of a revolver cocking. Alarmed, I looked in that direction and observed a scruffy-looking trapper pointing a sizeable hog-leg pistol out the window at an empty whiskey bottle on a stump. The deafening indoor shot rang out, and the bottle shattered into the pile of glass from many others. Amazingly, this target shooting occurred with regularity, as I deduced that the consumer of each bottle was obliged to shoot the empty vessel to prove their marksmanship and sobriety. I noticed that not far beyond the direction of the stump was a log cabin. I sincerely hoped that the cabin had thick logs, and that it was unoccupied.

There was another startling sound within the cacophony of slurred human voices—and it was blood-curdling. I noticed that many of the bar patrons had bleeding hands, but it wasn't from arm wrestling or fighting, as the blood oozing from the backs of their hands was from multiple, deep gashes. Cautiously, I investigated by maneuvering through the crowd toward the direction of the guttural howls. With an effort, I came to see the source of the frightening shrieks, for in a corner I observed a hissing and spitting lynx cub confined within a cage. Even though it was young, the huge dog-sized cat was formidable as it paced within the round, four-foot-diameter confinement. I noticed that this cage had a domed top, like an old-fashioned birdcage, only its construction was far more substantial, with widely spaced, rusty bars of thick steel. Dangling from a leather thong, at the center of the dome and just about a foot above the lynx's head, was a gold coin. Another crude, hand-painted sign hung on the wall above it, stating: A SAWBUCK A CHANCE. It then occurred to me that this was a cruel and dangerous form of Adirondack gambling. The deal was that a recklessly brave and usually drunk patron would post a ten-dollar piece with the bartender for a chance to stick his hand in the cage and snatch the gold coin. Actually, I observed that the gambler could have as many chances as they could endure, but usually they quit after receiving the first deep gushing wound. But when they gave up, the house got the sawbuck. Occasionally, two men would put up their money to tag-team the frenzied lynx, hoping that one would be successful and split the prize, which I estimated to be about fifty dollars. So far, the house was in no danger of losing. The wild and tormented cat would whirl and slash with claws at blinding speed, shredding their flesh and often leaving deep puncture wounds in their hands from unseen, cobra-quick bites. Drunk and stupefied men were no match for the cat's lightning-flash reflexes, but still, the cruelty of this enraged me.

It was also eerie, that aside from my brief interaction with the barkeep, I was unacknowledged and virtually invisible. Even my father, who sat drinking glass after glass of (what I now believed to be) locally made whiskey, didn't recognize my presence. I was alone in a crowd of drunk and pugnacious men. There were no women, which is probably why these guys were so quick to fight each other. And eventually, it happened.

Sometimes you can see the future even if you're stuck in the past. I knew bad things were about to happen, but it really didn't take an analyst to figure this out, especially given the nature of the tavern's clientele, along with their knives, axes, and firearms, all mixing with straight whiskey. It seemed the bar's patrons briefly achieved a level of spirited socialized intoxication and then quickly passed through that level and on to one of individual warfare. These days men drank together for comradery and to have a good time, but as soon as they got there, they destroyed it by fighting—with anyone, and for any reason.

As my father was tipping up yet another glass, a stinky trapper, smelling of fox urine, bellied up to the bar and bumped into his drinking arm, causing a minor spill of the cloudy, brown liquor on the bar. While the spilled liquid was quickly absorbed by the rough-sawn pine slab, my father noted the diminished level of his glass, and without hesitation, and while remaining seated, he cold-cocked the offending trapper with a left hook of his non-drinking arm. My father's lightning-quick response surprised me probably as much as it did the now unconscious trapper. I couldn't fathom how someone so drunk could execute such a fast, violent, and aggressive technique. Even more perplexing was that my father returned to his drink and resumed its consumption as if nothing had happened. But this was all that was required for pandemonium to break out.

It was as though the bell for the first round had rung. On cue, almost everyone, except for me, my father, and the barkeep, began punching, kicking, and grappling with each other. There was neither organization nor discernment to this combat. I noticed that even acquaintances fought each other as if they were lifelong foes. Often two men would gang up against one man, and as soon as he was subdued, they would turn on each other. I saw that Charlie was being pummeled while he was helplessly restrained in a headlock by a Paul Bunyan-sized logger. Upon hearing Charlie's cries for help, my father gazed briefly in his direction, but he appeared unconcerned and resumed drinking. Another man, however, rescued Charlie by breaking a stool over Mr. Bunyan's head. The huge logger released his headlock and collapsed on the floor. But as soon as Charlie regained his freedom, he kicked his rescuer in the groin and continued to kick his prostrate body. This was absolutely amazing, and while I enjoyed the spectacle of watching a Hollywood western-style bar fight in real time, I realized that neither my father nor I would be a spectator for long. I needed to get my father out of this precarious hellhole before he got hurt. But Father showed no willingness to leave. In fact, amid the melee, he was trying to get the bartender's attention to order up another bottle. I honestly believed my father had expended his one and only defensive move and would be an easy target for a barstool or a broken bottle attack. Luckily, as if it were written in some code of conduct for Adirondack bar fighting, no one drew a firearm, an axe, or even a knife, but I wasn't sure how long that would last. I had to get us out of here.

But before I did, my conservationist ethics required that I do something, and that was to set that poor lynx free. But its cage was so bulky and heavy that my juvenile stature couldn't carry it, and even if I could, the angry lynx would slash me to ribbons through its widely spaced bars. Therefore, I realized that the best I could do for the frenzied wildcat was to open its cage. But to give it a fighting chance, I first snapped closed the rusty lock that secured the long gun rack. I also removed its key and tossed it out of the window and into the pile of broken glass. I reasoned that these guys were way too drunk for accurate handgun fire, and the cat was too quick for their knives or axes. Next, to avoid getting punched, I crawled low on the floor to the lynx's cage and cautiously rotated it so the door faced the open window. But as soon as I pulled the hinge pins, the lynx burst through the door and leaped onto the back of a brawling man. Even while being pain-numbed by whiskey, the man howled as razor-sharp cat claws sunk deep into his flesh. But in a flash, the cat jumped from him and onto the back of another. More screaming ensued, and the fracas became even more pronounced as the lynx worked its way through the crowd, pouncing from man to man, adding to the mayhem. But this disturbance created a diversion and a safe path to extract my semi-comatose father. As I spied a clear way from the bar to the open door, I grabbed my father's non-drinking arm and pulled him off his stool. To my surprise, he didn't protest as he staggered in tow, but I noticed his other hand was still death-gripping the nearly empty whiskey bottle. With some difficulty, I loaded him aboard our wagon, where he collapsed in its bed. I quickly untied our horse, but before I said "gitty-up" I had another thing to do—and that was to set that damn bear free.

Apparently, I didn't have an accurate perspective of its size from our wagon because as I cautiously approached, it surprised me at how large the boar bear was. Just one bat from his massive, long-clawed paws and I wouldn't need to worry about getting back to the present. But the big bruin remained asleep as I unscrewed the shackle that secured the choke-chain around its neck. I could tell from its furless ring he had been captive for some time, probably since a cub. I realized that during this age, people thought differently about wildlife. *But why would anyone ever do this to such a magnificent creature?* From the chain's distant end, I gave it a tug to wake the bear and to hasten his escape, but to my great surprise, the bear got up on all fours and ran into the tavern's open door. At this, I realized that the imprinted bear was looking for his master, whom apparently he found and defended. I heard intense screaming from within the bar as the bear joined the brawl.

Through this adventure, I had learned much about Adirondack history, but I wanted to get out of this time trip because this had been a painful lesson. Also, I had a premonition I might not survive this session to tell the tale around next year's AB 101 campfire—assuming that there was another one for me. Also, I was in the wrong form because this was the era of "might makes right," and I wasn't very mighty, as I was an adult stuck in a child's body. While my experience and intellect helped me survive, I had a child's stature and, consequently, only a child's rights—which were nothing. Children were mere servants. Testament to this was that my father, noting my ability, was quick to add complexity to my chores without regard to their danger. His only concern was that I survived the task, and he predicated this on the necessity of my continued performance. Child abuse was neither a law, nor even a concept yet. Likewise, there were no daycare centers, no baby Zumba classes, no junior yoga gyms, nor child self-esteem camps. Doting parenting, helicoptering soccer moms, and effeminate, caring fathers had not yet evolved during this age. In this place, it was the wrong time to be a child, with anyone feeling free to give me a knee-buckling crack on the head just in case I did something. The problem for me was that the only way back to the present was in the cabin's cellar, and there were many miles of woods, streams, and treacherous trails between us. *Hell, I wasn't even sure if I could find my way back.*

~*~

Lucky for me the horse knew the way, just like the verse in that silly song. *Who knew autonomous driving vehicles had been around for years!* We got to the foundation just as night fell, and a warm nostalgic feeling and sense of place overcame me upon seeing the cabin in the early evening moonlight. I woke Father and led his stumbling, semi-comatose visage into the cabin. I removed his shoes, belt, and knife, stripped off his shirt and pants, but left him clothed in his union suit, which I didn't think he ever took off. I helped him into his bunk and started a small fire in the fireplace to take the chill off. When his snoring became rhythmic, and I was reasonably sure he wasn't going to vomit, I went out to the wagon to retrieve his rifle and knapsack. The crescent moon had set, but the stars that lit the clear sky seemed close enough to touch. It was another beautiful Adirondack night as I unharnessed our horse and secured him in the paddock. I made sure he had extra food and water for he had been a most trusty servant during this long day.

I returned to a pleasantly warmed cabin and took advantage of the fire's glowing coals by putting a pot of stew on it. This wilderness stew, which my father had taught me to make, was merely a concoction of smoked venison, beans, and salt water, but it would provide nourishment when he awoke. I also unpacked his knapsack and found the wad of bills that were the aim of today's adventure. To my surprise, he had $80 left, even after all that hard drinking at Gruffy's. As I believed, this was more money than he made in a year from maple syrup or trapping. I knew, like most men of this time, that he was self-reliant, but I found it perplexing he could survive on such a meager income. Especially since he grew no crops and had to go trad'n' for supplies in Saranac Lake. While this concerned me, I went about stowing his gear and preparing for my final exit. I made sure that his pipe was out and stowed it along with his tobacco pouch (made from a buck's scrotum) in its place on the fireplace mantle. I left his brass-cased compass, skinning knife, and rifle ammo in the pack but secured his cash in the tin kept in the cupboard for his maple syrup sales. As I added the wad to the nearly empty tin, I noticed that the many brown bottles of maple syrup that lined the cupboard shelves looked a lot like the whiskey bottles of Gruffy's. Intrigued, I pulled the cork out of one and took a swig—it wasn't maple syrup. This discovery was yet another enigma, as aside from his celebratory foray at the tavern, my father was not a drinking man. *So why did he have so much whiskey stocked?*

While pondering this, I took another walk around of the area. I checked on our horse and the oxen. I brought in more firewood, even though the hopper was full, and I checked on the pot of gruel I had made, which would probably end up becoming my father's breakfast. Everything seemed in order, and although I tried, I couldn't think of another thing to do. It was time to go. *Why was I forestalling it?* Could it be, believe it or not, that I cared for the man that was my father? Even though he was a cruel and merciless man, over these few days we had bonded, and now I fretted about what would happen to him when I left for the present. *Would the child's form I inhabited continue? Would it still be able to provide this same level of care for my father, or would it devolve to be a child of less than a dozen years?* I realized that even thinking such things was weird, but as I say, I had become used to this new definition of weird.

With resolve and with care, I ambled down the creaky stairs with a dimly flickering slush lamp barely lighting my way. When I could feel the cellar's dirt floor afoot, I made my way to the stone slab shelf and set the smelly light upon it. I positioned my hands on each side of the thick stone for a good purchase and blew out the lamp. Lucky for me, my childlike form didn't have to remove the shelf; I only had to shake it as if threatening to dislodge it. This act was apparently enough to trigger the temporal paradox. It took all of my strength to nudge the stone, but my effort was successful, and I felt myself expand as I returned to the present. I was so grateful to be back in my adult body, but a half glimpse of something in the cellar's corner troubled me. For, just as the lamp extinguished, I spotted a large, conical copper vessel with a coil of thin piping spiraling from it and into a keg.

~*~

I got to camp just as morning twilight was breaking. But even from a distance in the predawn darkness, I could tell that something was askew. For one thing, the door was open and there was stuff scattered in front of it. Being cautious, I hunkered down, using a fallen tree for cover, and watched, and waited for better light. For all that I knew, a bear had just ransacked the camp and was still in there.

About half of an hour later, the sun was cresting over Moose Mountain, and I could see that most of my provisions and gear had been thrown out of the camp's open door. This wasn't the work of a bear. The troopers had been here looking for me, and they wanted me to know it. I'm guessing that they were hoping I'd get spooked by having my hideout discovered and turn myself in. I thought this tactic was pretty dumb, but it probably worked for more than a few mutts they were chasing. While I gave surrendering some thought, especially given the non-serious nature of my crime (I had hurt no one—all I did was fill a guy's Beemer with water, right?), I was downright opposed to giving Fast Freddy or Marlene the satisfaction of seeing me do the perp-walk. My lam would continue until I ran out of room to run, which in the Adirondacks is kinda hard. But I knew where I had to go. I would move my hideaway to the foundation.

I figured that they might return soon, so I hastily picked through my gear adrift, sorting it into piles of necessities and piles of things that would be nice to have. Before long, my necessities were more than I could carry in my largest pack basket. Consequently, I'd be leaving a lot of good things on the ground. Now, I'd really be roughing it, and that sucked!

I thought about making a travois and dragging additional gear, but the drag marks would make my trail too easy to follow. The virtue of the foundation was that it was difficult to find, and I didn't want to lose that advantage. Hell, I still had a hard time finding it, and I'd been there dozens of times. Thinking about this made me realize that Marlene must have told the troopers about Earl's camp. Although she had been there only once, her real estate prowess must have enabled her to give them its description and location: "It's a quaint, rustically elegant, waterfront bungalow, sequestered in a gated community, amid primal forested land on a private road." (Translation: it's a ramshackle shack, near a creek, in the woods, on a jeep trail with a chain across.)

They wouldn't have such an easy time finding the foundation though. I imagined they would enlist the help of my former employer—the DEC. The troopers often called upon the rangers when they needed to find someone who wanted to be found, like a lost hiker. But when the troopers wanted to find someone who didn't want to be found, like a fugitive (like moi), they called upon Mother Nature's hitmen, the ECOs. As I mentioned, the environmental conservation officers were the descendants of the legendary game protectors, and unfortunately for me, they had inherited their man-tracking skills. So I packed my basket with several cans of beans, coffee, and my Primus stove, so I wouldn't need a cooking fire that would give away my position. I also took my goose down sleeping bag and my Eureka pup tent, which I found chucked in the debris field. But there was one more thing I needed—a shoot'n' iron.

I had left Grampa's old hog-leg revolver locked in my truck, parked at the trailhead to camp. It would be crazy to go near my truck because it was likely staked out. So I pawed around the debris until I found an old claw hammer and headed to the outhouse. The troopers had unnecessarily searched that too, ripping the door off its hinges, and had even tupped my last roll of toilet paper down the hole. Assholes! But there was something important that their refined search skills had failed to detect—missing interior space. I went to work on the back wall pulling rusty nails from the weathered boards until I removed the false wall that concealed a gun cabinet. Earl was a WWII veteran, and consequently, he didn't trust that our right to bear arms would always be upheld. His distrust was likely the result of witnessing this happen in Europe, and the easy time the Nazis had invading these unarmed countries. So he hid a few of his beauties in the last place most people would look—an old, dilapidated, and very stinky outhouse.

Between the rough-cut timbers were three choices: an M-1 Springfield, a drilling (that's an over and under, rifle/shotgun combination), and a double-barreled Gibraltar shotgun. All were preserved magnificently by being wrapped in waxed burlap and with the metal parts smeared with a light coat of Cosmoline. My first choice was the M-1, but Earl, being true to his safety code, didn't secrete any ammunition with the guns. I was sure that there was another hiding place for the ammo but didn't have time to look for it. I remembered that there were a few rounds of birdshot in the camp, so hoping that the troopers hadn't taken it, I grabbed the Gibraltar. Imagine my surprise when I broke it open to check the bores and two brass-hulled buckshot rounds ejected. I reasoned that, since they were all brass and wouldn't corrode, Earl must have left them to keep moisture out of the chambers. I wiped the Cosmoline from the shotgun, and when I reloaded, I noticed that each shell had 1956 etched on their casing. They were antiques, but in my experience these brass-hulled shells maintained their integrity. My presumed need for a firearm wasn't so I could get into a gunfight with the law. I needed a gun because I was camping in the wilderness, and a man needs to be prepared. If I ran into it, thanks to Earl, I had two chances to get out of it, *whatever "it" may be.*

CHAPTER 12

The days were long, and the nights were even longer, as I had little to do except hunker down and hide while camping. No excursions, no campfire, and even no s'mores. Since my bright green pup tent didn't blend well with the rusty, post-peak foliage, I set it up within the foundation, which was kind of creepy and didn't give me a view of anything. Fall was in the air, and there was a chill to the wind, especially at night when the coywolves would ensure that I didn't sleep by singing their mournful songs. When I was tucked safely within the cabin, their calls seemed soothing and sleep-inducing, but now, being separated from them by only a thin sheet of nylon, their howls were menacing. When I did drift off, I'd have dreams of salivating coywolves circling the tent, waiting for me to sleep so they could pounce and tear into my unprotected flesh. Consequently, the double-barreled Gibraltar became my sleeping companion. I realized that this primal fear of being eaten came from reading too many Jack London novels during my youth, but it was real now.

By being an arrow target and needing a shield, I had discovered how to return to the present; but I hadn't yet learned how to go back into the past. And these days, this was equally painful, as I was bored to death and down to my last can of beans. I needed a distraction and desperately wanted another time-trip adventure, but I couldn't just will it. I reviewed my movements that had triggered previous trips and attempted to reenact them, but none worked. And I tried everything: shaking the stone slab, poking and pawing around the foundation walls

—I even tried meditation—nada! *I was stuck.*

Verily I shivered as I took short excursions in search of something edible. Not realizing how long I would be laming it, I hadn't packed enough warm clothing. The seasons had changed quickly, and I wasn't sure if the North Country had skipped fall and went straight into winter. I beefed-up the insulation of the pup tent (wait—what insulation?) by layering moss and strips of bark over the top of it; and since it was nestled within the foundation, it was reasonably well-protected from the wind. But I couldn't stay in the tent all day. I had this deep, bone-numbing chill and wanted a fire so bad, that one night I risked making a small one. Earlier that day I had found some Indian cucumber (an edible root that resembles wild ginseng but tastes just like a cucumber. *Thank you, Dr. Torrance!)* Also, I had cut some fresh cambium from a recently fallen White Pine, which I roasted on the fire. The fire caramelized its sugary sap, making it taste, more or less, like a turpentine-flavored pancake. Since hunger is the world's best seasoning, I thought it was delicious, and now I could say that I was a real bark eater! The other much-appreciated benefit of risking a fire is that it kept those damn coywolves away. If only I hadn't been shivering so badly, I might have slept that night. I had remembered, too late, about rigging a fly to reflect the infrared heat from the fire's embers toward the tent. I would do that the next time, but I knew my paranoid mind wouldn't let me make another fire unless I was too cold to think properly.

The old saying: "be careful what you wish for" had little meaning these days because I wished so hard to go back—even as an amoeba or any other form of pond life. I was miserable, hungry, and sleep deprived. But even more than all those minor inconveniences, I was freezing! In fact, I thought I was experiencing the foreshadowing effects of hypothermia when I felt woozy as I reached for the stone slab. I had been moving it around for days, even using it as a makeshift table, with no effect. Now at my wits-end, I was going to risk making another fire and was positioning the slab as a backstop reflector. Actually, this wasn't much of a risk because I had decided that if I survived the night, in the morning I would turn myself in. Marlene and Freddy be damned, being alive is the best revenge!

But, turns out, I didn't have to surrender. As the walls of the foundation dissolved, I thought of another old saying: If you want to hear God laugh, tell him your plans.

~*~

As I felt myself take form, I cautiously looked around to surveil my situation. Thankfully, I saw that I had hands, *and not paws or flippers,* although they were grotesquely scarred like they had been burned. The palms were rough and callused, but the backs appeared to be raw with pink, puffy flesh exposed from wrist to knuckles. Without regard to their unsightly appearance, I was glad they were the hands of a man and not another child, and especially not a woman's hands. I took in my surroundings. I was standing in the middle of a drab room with various furnishings for sitting (*I think they called this a parlor*), with dark green wallpaper, but…I was warm. The source of my comfort was coming from a brown enameled stove that was standing along a windowless wall. I believe they used to call these monstrosities parlor stoves, and its smoke pipe exited through a plate in the wall. I discerned that coal was its fuel because of the bucketful that my hands were manipulating. As though I knew exactly what I was doing, I opened the draft, opened the side door, and carefully banked a few shovelfuls of coal within the firebox. I closed the door, and when the mica insert of the stove's front grill glowed bright, I reset the draft. While I didn't have complete information, I was melding into my new form quickly, as something told me I was leaving this domicile to go to work. But where, and for whom?

On my way out of the parlor, I walked past another dark papered wall on which two sepia-toned photographs hung. They were in wooden oval frames, and one was of a young man in an old-fashioned army uniform and another of a regal woman in a long white dress, sitting on a chair in—you guessed it—a dark and dismal room. I reasoned that the guy was me.

This revelation prompted me to find a mirror, so I searched for a bathroom within the tiny domicile but only found a closet with a chamber pot; since the only purpose for this room was elimination, thankfully there was no mirror within it. But during my quest, I took stock of my quarters. There was an open area off of the parlor, which apparently served as a kitchen and dining room. A small wooden table, with only two chairs and an oversized wood-fired cooking stove within, confirmed my belief. I deduced the stove was converted to modern coal gas by the decorative plate above it that covered the hole in the wall where the smoke pipe used to exit. In fact, most of the lights in the dwelling were gas lanterns; however, there was one Edison-style light bulb hanging from a wire in the parlor. This place had electric power for lighting but no receptacles, so I guessed that plug-in conveniences hadn't been invented yet. Aside from the chamber closet, there was only one other room in the abode, a bedroom, and I heard soft, rhythmic breathing from within.

There was a woman asleep in a compact, two-person bed, and there was also a dark wooden dresser with a hazy mirror mounted on it. Quietly, I observed the woman's ample features without disturbing her slumber and assessed that she was the same woman in that "antique" photograph. *But who was she in relation to me?* Next, I ventured to look in the mirror, and what I saw amazed and pleased me.

I was a male in my early thirties, and not too bad looking. I was clean-shaven, except for a thick bushy mustache, and had short brown hair cut in a military style. Additionally, I looked to be about the same height as that of my present form (just shy of six feet), and likewise, I appeared to be trim, with flesh well laid on. *But on the left side of my neck there was that same pink blister scarring that was on my hands.* I dressed in a full-pack green military uniform. *But with a gray cardigan sweater?* The sweater seemed more like an overcoat, being double thickness wool with leather elbow and shoulder patches. It was warm and heavy, and it even smelled like a sheep. *But it didn't match the uniform?* I unbuttoned the sweater to check things out and observed a diagonal cross-body strap leading to a thick brown leather belt. Hanging off the right side of the belt was a flap-over holster; on the left side were a dozen huge brass cartridges, poking out of leather loops. I was armed, but why?

Continuing my exploration, I undid the flap fastener, which was just a brass pin poking through a hole in the leather, and observed the buckhorn grips of a big Colt revolver. Nice! I buttoned my sweater and continued toward the door where I found a coatrack from which an olive-green cowboy hat hung, and leaning against it was a lever-action carbine. I recognized it as a Winchester 1873. Something told me to collect both items before heading out, so I donned the hat, slung the rifle, and opened the door.

The door opened to the outside and down a flight of rickety stairs which egressed into an unpaved back alley. *So I was in a small city, or more likely a village.* I continued to follow my instincts around the stairs to an open shed-like structure, created by enclosing the underside of the stairway. Nestled under the structure appeared to be an extreme fat-tire mountain bicycle, only its muddy tires were white, not just whitewalls, and made entirely from white rubber. In the dark enclosure, I could see only the front of the bicycle, but I noticed that there was a beat-up leather scabbard attached to the right side of the deeply swept-back handlebars. I guessed correctly that it was for the Winchester, so I slipped the rifle in it and pulled the bike out of the shadows. It was then I noticed how heavy it was, and that was because set low within its frame was a cast iron V-twin engine. Behold, it was a Harley!

I also noticed that stenciled in white lettering below the orange Harley-Davidson logo was PROPERTY OF THE FISHERIES, GAME AND FOREST COMMISSION. Upon this observation, a swirl of knowledge flooded my brain.

And thus, I came to know the background of my situation:

The year was 1923.

My name was Henry Hawkins, and I had served as a soldier during the Great War, but now I was a game protector for the Fisheries, Game, and Forest Commission.

I lived in the hotel room I had just left, in the Village of Saranac Lake, with my wife, Ana.

The conveyance I first thought was a bicycle was my year-round patrol vehicle. The commission fit these war-surplus motorcycles with a sidecar and a canvas contraption called a "winter windshield." I came to learn that the commission issued motorcycles or horses for patrol. But, if issued a horse, the food and board for it would come out of my salary of eight dollars per month.

While I assessed this scenario, I came to know more pieces of it, and actually liked it. Here was a time period that I knew something about, and it was civilized. No more hanging from a tree, dodging arrows, or getting clunked on the head. All I had to do was be a husband (*a previous role that I had been relatively lousy in, but this was my chance for a do-over*) and play game cop—an occupation that my wildlife science background would meld with. A piece of cake! But, like most things in life, nothing is as easy as it seems.

The first order of business was to get my patrol vehicle started. In my present life, I had always dreamed of owning a Harley, but now that I had one, I wasn't so sure that I based this dream on disillusionment. For one thing, I looked for a starter button but could only find a single bicycle pedal on the machine's right side. I knew this was the kick-starter, but when I attempted to use it, I nearly got bucked over the handlebars. I settled down and massaged my sore leg as more information came. A revelation then occurred—along with switching on the ignition, I needed to retard the timing, turn on the fuel tap, and set the choke. Upon accomplishing these tasks, the engine started on the third kick, but it didn't sound like any Harley I had ever heard. It had a harsh, dog-bark exhaust note and a lot of mechanical noises, but something told me that this was normal. The next undertaking I had to master was getting this rumbling beast into gear, for the clutch was a rat-trap affair on the left floorboard, and also, the gearshift was on the left side of the gas tank. I thought this setup was somewhat dangerous, but people were coordinated during this era and ergonomics weren't yet thought of.

With the wildly vibrating machine ready to go, I fastened the chinstrap of my cowboy hat (*that I would come to know as a "Stetson"*), shifted into first, released the clutch, and chugged away. I negotiated the alleyway and briefly stopped at its intersection with the unpaved street, which I recognized as Broadway. A few things looked familiar, such as the building that would house the Downtowne Grille, but presently, it was a department store called Ginnegan's. Actually, I recognized a lot of the old buildings and structures. While their names were unrecognizable, their robust, pre-WWI construction would ensure that they lasted beyond my present time. However, the one structure that would not endure is the hotel I lived in. They called it Berkeley House, and the owners had originally built it as a "cure cottage" with plenty of open-air porches. The fresh air provided by these Adirondack cure cottage porches afforded relief and occasional remission from the symptoms of tuberculosis. However, now that recreating in the Adirondack Mountains had become fashionable, sick people sitting in steamship lounges on a hotel's porch was bad for business. Which is probably why another hand-painted sign hung under the Berkeley House sign stated "NO INVALIDS." Lucky for the hotel proprietors, Edward Trudeau's new clinic took the pressure off of their establishments by providing lodging and focused treatment for hundreds of those afflicted. But it was a little creepy to know that in a decade they would discover an antibiotic that would eliminate the need for Adirondack air to treat tuberculosis.

Equally uncanny was that I could see that Berkeley House's replacement, the "Hotel Saranac," was under construction. This ultra-modern art deco hotel would take so many of Berkeley's established clients that it would make rebuilding doubtful after the minor fire that would befall this hotel—in two years.

In awe and with great amazement, I continued my tour through the village. On the streets, there were many horse-drawn conveyances, but few motorcars—and most of them I identified as Ford Model Ts. But the sparse traffic wasn't an issue, which was fortunate for me since I was still learning to master the archaic controls of this motorcycle. But so far, the most significant problem I encountered was navigating around the piles of horse-plop. I found out, the hard way, this motorcycle's skimpy fenders were as ineffective as its brakes. I needed to get out of town, and I knew where I wanted to go.

It reckoned that at least fifty years had elapsed since I had been to the foundation—which was in another life. I correctly reasoned that my current form was too young to be the child I had left in the cabin that night. Given all the cracks on the head he would have received during his adolescence, if he was still alive, the old man was probably providing some village with an idiot now. I was also fairly sure that the guy who played my father was pushing up daisies, but I had to see.

Like a moth to the flame!

I was pleasantly surprised the road to the foundation was relatively clear of fallen trees and the ground was dry. Someone had recently maintained this path, as there was sap flowing from fresh blazes cut on the pines. *But who would do this? Was someone still living in the cabin?*

I was glad the road was in good shape because the Harley was no dirt bike. The cabin, however, was a different story. One look answered my question about its habitation. There was a substantial dead spruce lying on its roof, causing it to sag. I could also see several areas where branches had penetrated the roof, leaving large holes for the weather to enter. The door was ajar and hanging by only one of its three hinges. Since I had last seen the cabin, someone had upgraded the windows from greased paper to glass, but two out of the four were broken. As I approached, I observed a lot of animal tracks leading in and out of the half-open door, and some of them were fairly large bear paw prints. Not knowing what creatures were lurking within, I drew the big Colt and held it by my side as I entered.

The interior was a mess, with pine needles, animal scat, and small bones scattered around the filthy floor. But I saw no signs of recent human activity. *At least not for the last couple of decades.* Being reasonably confident that the cabin was bear free, I holstered my gun. A thick layer of decaying pollen covered every horizontal surface, with cobwebs bridging most of their transitions to the loosely chinked log walls. In a moment of curiosity, I looked into the half-open cupboard where I had previously discovered all those bottles of whiskey—all were gone. But another upgrade had occurred in my absence; beeswax candles had replaced the stinky flesh-fueled slush lamps. Embedded into the fireplace mantle were several melted candles. I deduced that this lighting advancement had taken place many years ago because a thick coating of melted wax covered the mantle's formerly roughhewn surface. *Apparently, fire prevention wasn't yet a consideration.* I broke a candle free, lit it, and took the wobbly stairs into the cellar.

Unlike the topsides, the stone foundation was in good shape. A reflective sense of awe, with maybe a touch of nostalgia, washed over me as I thought of the many eons and time progressions I had witnessed this foundation prevail over. I was on hallowed ground. As I looked around, I realized that the distilling vessel and its apparatus were missing. All that copper was probably turned into pennies by now. The illuminated arc of the candlelight didn't extend very far, and yet I was half-blinded by its bright flame. I had to navigate cautiously along the relatively uncluttered perimeter. As I was noticing how dry the dirt floor felt, I bumped into something solid, and there it was—the stone slab shelf. It was still cantilevered securely into the corner but now a half-burned candle sat upon it. Its sight relieved my anxiety and gave me a sense of freedom by knowing my return ticket to the present was available. But I had no desire to touch it. *I wasn't ready yet!*

After checking the damp, rotten bedding in the loft where I used to sleep, I headed outside for fresh air. I took in the surroundings and saw that the horse paddock was still standing, but the rock-walled smokehouse had collapsed into a near-perfect moss-covered pyramid. The split log fence that surrounded the clearing around the cabin had disintegrated. In its place were rusty strands of barbed wire, a trickle-down technology from the use of concertina wire during trench warfare. The strands were haphazardly strung and mostly lying on the ground as their support posts had rotted and were replaced by many small balsams. I took the short walk to the vernal pond and surveyed the cemetery. Alongside my mother's stick cross stood two additional ones: a large log cross for a guy named Hezekiah, and a smaller one for a boy named Joshua. I never even knew their names and yet I lived with and within them. *How did they die and who buried them?* As I hiked back to my mount, a profound sadness overcame me.

I motored back into town and prepared to embrace my new life.

CHAPTER 13

My home life was pretty darn good, even in that tiny hotel suite. Ana was the consummate homemaker, and while she wasn't a beauty, like the verse in that fifties song, "she sure could cook!" Ana could turn any scrap of fish, fowl, or game I brought home into a gourmet meal. She also kept an immaculate house which was no easy task, considering we didn't have running water or a flushing toilet. Ana was also a woman of few words, and when she did speak, it was with a thick accent that sounded German. It took me a while to understand her, but I understood why she didn't talk much, because Americans had ostracized Germans after the war. That she was a Serbian and served as a nurse at an English field hospital had no meaning. This hospital (*which was in a tent*) is where Henry first met her, when Nurse Ana tended to his mustard gas wounds. (*This memory, although vague, came after staring at those pink scars on my neck and wrists too many times*). A year after the war, Ana's family emigrated to America, and she became a citizen. The Adirondack Mountains must have reminded the family of the Dinaric Alps of their homeland because they settled in the area that would be known as the High Peaks. Henry and Ana became reacquainted when he discovered she was the teacher for the Bloomingdale Schoolhouse. Ana had to stop teaching when they married because teachers weren't allowed to marry back then. Remarkably, she was the sole teacher for all grades of the schoolhouse. I had to wonder, though, how the hell could those poor kids understand her?

As expected, I was a natural for the game protector job. I

knew right where to look for trouble, but since I didn't have any law enforcement experience, I was a little behind the curve on what to do when I found it. However, I found this situation to be the same with my counterpart-coworkers, as most of them were not former lawmen either. In fact, the commission hired most of them because of their poaching prowess (it takes a poacher to catch a poacher was the commission's decree), but true to Teddy Roosevelt's directive, they were thorough woodsmen. They were also tough men because dispositions for law violations were more often settled by fist fights in the woods than they were in court. I found that there wasn't an initial training program for this job either. When they hired a new game protector, he received a letter directing him to catch the train to Albany, take his oath, and pick up his equipment. After receiving a patrol sector assignment, often comprising several counties, they provided training for the new protector in piecemeal sessions. Mostly it was about enforcing new laws and patrol methods. Training in the "use of force" wasn't among these topics, which was dumbfounding considering we carried guns and made arrests. Near as I could tell, there were only a half dozen game protectors stationed in the Adirondacks. We rarely saw one another unless they ordered us to attend a training session. These orders usually came via the U.S. Mail service, but occasionally, the regional supervisor would inform us in person. I think this was in part so the supervisor could verify that each man was fit for duty and reasonably sober. One day I received a letter from my supervisor informing me I was to meet with him at the Ray Brook Headquarters on the first Wednesday of the following month. Not knowing how formal these meetings were, I polished all of my leather while Ana pressed my uniforms and cut my hair. I cleaned my guns, changed the Harley's oil, and gave it a bath. I was ready for inspection.

The letter stated that I was to be at the regional headquarters "no later than on or about noon." As Ray Brook came into view, my pocket watch showed it was 11:30, so I reckoned that

I had time to look around. As I chugged into the U-shaped dirt driveway of the "Little Albany" outpost, the similarity of it to the present New York State agency campus surprised me. I saw the new long-house barracks of the state troopers. Behind it were horse stables along with a corral, its perimeter being formed by that ubiquitous barbed wire. There were several troopers tending the horses, and I waved to them as I rolled past. I noticed they wore the same gray cardigan sweater as me. *No wonder it was gray and not green; it was a trooper uniform.* Here we game protectors were the first statewide police agency, and we were wearing hand-me-downs from the newly formed but well-funded state troopers. We had lousy leadership way back then.

Demoralized, I continued riding to the future site of the Department of Environmental Conservation Great-Camp-style building, where the tiny log cabin of the Fisheries, Game, and Forest Commission stood. I noted that missing from the scenery was the Adirondack Park Agency headquarters. I realized this agency wouldn't be created for another fifty years, and when it was, most of the local folks would wish that it had stayed "missing."

A ruggedized Model T truck was parked in front of the FGF cabin. I reasoned that this must be my boss's ride because they only issued supervisors cars. I observed smoke curling from the chimney and drafting down the roof, indicating a recently kindled fire. He had just arrived, and since I had announced my arrival by the Harley's rumbling, I had no reason to dally. I stood at attention and pounded on the door, three times as they taught me in the military.

I heard a familiar voice say, "C'mon en, Henry."

As I entered, I saw a man dressed in the same garb as me, but I recognized him as the old Adirondack guide. I swear it was him, although it was a considerably cleaned-up version in a game protector uniform. Gone was the long beard and unkempt hair, but he kept his mustache and sported the same bowl-head haircut I did, which was the current post-war style. He was sitting behind an olive green metal desk and was pouring himself a stipple of brown liquid from a flask into a coffee cup. On his collar tabs was the rank insignia for an army captain, so I saluted.

He stowed the container in a desk drawer and said, "Knock that shit off, and take a seat, Mas... ah, Henry." *Holy crap, I think he almost called me Mason!*

This was beyond bizarre, but here he was—the returning character from the past, and the present! Had he found the foundation too? Without being asked, I handed him my lengthy Monthly Report of Apprehensions, which he filed without even looking at. *I was kinda proud of that report, especially since, in reality, I was new to the job.* As he sipped from the cup, he made small talk, asking about the fish run and about Ana and such. After a few minutes of this preamble, he came to the reason for the meeting.

He said, "Next week you're going to Plattsburgh for training. It's at that new Federal Office Building. I have to send the whole damn region, so you'll get to meet the protectors from the other backcountry outposts. The session's supposed to last the week, but I doubt that it'll take more than one long day."

The boss had informed me of the "who, where, and when" of the mission, but the "what" was missing. So I logically asked, "Sir, what is the training about?"

He said, "Ain't about a damn thing! You guys is getting deputized as treasury agents—that's all."

Holy cow, I forgot that this was the Prohibition Era! From his cranky response, I deduced that my captain supervisor, or whatever he was, was not a proponent of the Eighteenth Amendment. *The flask should have been a clue.*

After being dismissed—uninspected and unsupervised—I motored around my patrol area looking for violations. It was late autumn when I left the present, but here, it was early spring. So it seemed like a good day to check fishermen along the Ausable River.

~*~

The training session in Plattsburgh didn't even last as long as my supervisor predicted. I had arrived before 0800 and here I was shaking hands and saying goodbye to my coworkers by noon, which was good because Saranac Lake was a long ride on an antique motorcycle. "See ya in the spring," seemed to be the catchphrase, and I wondered if it would really be a whole year before we'd meet again.

The pace of the presentation was brisk, and thankfully, no one delayed its completion by asking stupid questions. The presenter was a eulogizing treasury agent named Alonzo Baines, who wore a real cowboy hat (even when indoors) and a tan suit with one of those skinny string ties. I got the impression he was from out west, or that he just wanted to be a cowboy. Agent Baines went on (with a twangy western accent) about the evils of alcohol, and how drinking and drunkenness had prevented America from fully participating in the war effort. Wow! While I had only a vague memory of my past self as Henry in the trenches, I recalled from my present-day high school history that almost five million men had served during World War I. *What the hell was he talking about?!* I found it exceedingly difficult to refer to "World War I" as just "the war," or as "The Great War." I realized this was what they called it because no one could envision there would ever be another world war. Fortunately for me, most people, especially the veterans, didn't talk much about it.

Treasury Agent Baines prattled on about how alcohol was costing society millions of dollars in law enforcement. I noted that he mentioned nothing about "treatment." He further stated that unscrupulous Canadian distillers were adding methanol to their raw booze to give it the necessary alcohol content. This immoral act was causing blindness, insanity, and death to unsuspecting American imbibers. Agent Baines directed that it was our duty to stop this terrible threat by patrolling trails, rivers, and back roads where this booze was covertly being transported from across the border. He additionally stated our deputy status authorized us to take decisive action and use all force necessary to prosecute these criminal rum runners. By that statement, I wasn't sure what he meant, but I knew what it meant to the other game protectors—by their rough-and-ready nature, it translated to mean frontier justice. Ironically, throughout Agent Baines' presentation, these guys were either asleep or displaying outright contention to his preaching. I suspected that most of them enjoyed an occasional drink and that those occasions occurred with regularity. But what they believed didn't matter because they were predacious lawmen—intoxicated more by the thrill of the hunt than by mere alcohol. They would enforce any law that satisfied their arrest addiction, even if they were the most prolific violator of that law.

At the conclusion of several hours of motivational speeches with little instruction, Agent Baines passed out badges. They looked like a US Marshal star with a circle around the points, along with the inscription DEPUTY UNITED STATES TREASURY AGENT. Agent Baines instructed us to wear them on the left breast of our outer garment, at all times. I stowed mine in my left shirt pocket. Perhaps it would stop a bullet.

~*~

So I didn't waste my valuable training, I patrolled various waterways of my sector with an eye for rum runners. I knew too well that the strong northerly current of the Saranac would effectively prevent any barge traffic, but it was a good ploy to check for fish traps. Occasionally, I even staked out the Lake Champlain Narrows at the future site of the Essex Ferry crossing. During those long nights, while bored out of my mind, I wondered why the military hadn't run a chain across the lake during the War of 1812, like they had on the Hudson at West Point during the Revolutionary War.

I stopped any truck that was heading south on a back road. This was no easy task on a motorcycle. While the bike's superior power made it easy to overtake a vehicle, its light weight made it an easy target for those who didn't want to stop—and most drivers didn't. More than once I unholstered the big Colt and threated to shoot out their tires to get a very begrudging compliance. Through all this, I never found any booze shipments, but I did uncover a lot of wildlife offenses, with which I was far more gratified. Having the burden of future knowledge, I knew we would repeal Prohibition in a scant ten years as a failed experiment that actually increased crime. I reckon that I couldn't help seeing a parallel with the present day prohibition on drugs.

But, like I mentioned, the violators didn't like getting arrested, and they often fought like hell. This brought me a lot of excitement and some harrowing scrapes.

One time I stopped an elderly man and woman who were driving a horse-drawn wagon with a canvas cover. I made the man pull back the canvas, revealing three out-of-season doe deer. Actually, this was a big deal because there was no season on a doe (dead doe deer don't breed, was the commission's decree), and since deer were pretty much extirpated from the Adirondacks because of market hunting, the penalty for this offense was significant. So I was keeping an extra close watch on the old guy as I was about to manacle him when I heard the unmistakable racking of a pump shotgun.

Shocked, I found myself staring into the big bore of an M97 trench gun, expertly wielded by the old woman I'd been ignoring. I couldn't think of a thing to do—that was, until I remembered a scene from an old western movie. I immediately drew the Colt, put it to the man's head—cocked it—and in my best John Wayne imitation, I said, "Ya shoot me, an' this peckerwood's a goner!"

Several tense minutes passed before she lowered the gun, after which I manacled them together, and to the wagon. I had them follow me to the county courthouse. I'm sure that it was a long ride for them, especially since they would likely go straight to jail—but they didn't. This was mostly because I advised the judge that they were heading toward their home with those deer, and not to a hotel where they could sell them. I also told him they needed food and didn't have much money (in the interest of both parties, I necessarily didn't mention that little Mexican standoff we had). So the judge seizes their shotgun (to be sold to pay their fine) and gives them the deer. I thought it was a fair judgment, especially since I knew in seventy years doe deer would over-populate the Adirondacks.

Another time I was coming back home from Lake Champlain late at night. As usual, I was dog tired after an exceptionally boring surveillance. As I jostled along the rutty dirt road, the old Harley's lantern flickered, and I realized that it was running out of kerosene. So before it went out, I stopped by a well-lit farmhouse to see if I could borrow some kerosene.

Before I tell the rest of this story, I should mention that I had fashioned a crude but effective muffler from a couple of tin cans for that loud-barking V-twin. I did this mostly to protect what was left of my hearing (I had a constant ringing in my ears, but it was probably the result of Henry's service during "the War"), and because I couldn't feature sneaking up on poachers with a machine that announced its presence from miles away. By the way, during our deputizing get-together, all of my fellow motor officers were envious of this new contraption.

Well, the muffler, along with my dim headlight, must have made for a stealth entrance because when I knocked on the un-latched door, it flew open and I saw two guys butchering a fawn on the kitchen table.

The old adage "that a handgun's only purpose is to fight your way back to your rifle, which you should have brought to the gunfight to begin with" came to mind during this fracas. I thought this because while one guy held me off by slashing at me with a butcher knife, the other guy reached for his rifle that was lying on the kitchen counter. Luckily, I had the advantage of surprise, which gave me a few precious seconds to make a tactical retreat and grab my rifle from the Harley's scabbard. Once I had the short-barreled Winchester in hand, I poked the muzzle into the doorway and rapidly fired several rounds into their ceiling. Our rifles and revolvers were chambered for the same cartridge, which was the bullet that won the West—the venerable 44-40 Winchester. This was a big bullet, with lots of propellant (black powder) behind it, and when you fired it into an enclosed space, like a small kitchen, the thunderous sound and overpressure were near equal to a modern-day flash-bang grenade. Also, the football of flame out of the Winchester's short barrel greatly added to the shock and awe. The stun result was dramatic. Both guys dropped their weapons, put their hands to their ears, and fell to their knees. This made "hooking them up" a lot easier than I had expected. Another thing I hadn't expected was that they had a telephone. It was in a large oak cabinet hanging from the wall—an antique, even back then. I had no idea if it worked, or even how it worked. Recalling old movies, I put the handset to my ear and heard a dial tone, but there was no dial; there was only this magneto crank on the cabinet's side.

So I turned the crank for a few seconds, and then I heard, "Essex Country Operator, may I help you?"

I remembered seeing an NE-6 next my boss's name on the duty roster, so I said, "Ah...yes, North Elba six, please."

Luckily, it was his phone number, and about an hour later I heard his truck rattle up to the farmhouse. We loaded the half-butchered fawn and the two mutts in the truck's open bed. I found some kerosene and topped off the Harley's lantern, per my original reason for stopping, and followed the Model T to the judge's house. Being woken up, the judge was not nearly as lenient with these guys as he was with the old couple, so we had to make a subsequent trip to the county jail. It was early morning by the time I got home.

A few nights after we settled this case, I caught two guys using one of these telephone magnetos to electro-fish. Again, I got home particularly late, and I expected Ana to be sleeping. Instead, she had this fancy dinner all laid out for me. I wondered what the occasion was but didn't have to wait long, for as soon as I sat down, she told me she was pregnant.

~*~

I almost blurted out "who's the father?" because it seemed having sex during this period was reserved for birthdays, and I hadn't one of those yet. But then again, I wasn't thinking about Henry's birthday, which was about a month before I had arrived. This was an entirely new experience for me, in any life, and more than a little scary. Now I had to think about providing for another human being.

My angst must have shown because Ana said, "Dinna vorry, everting vill vork out vight."

I mentioned one of my concerns, like my job that didn't pay well, and she replied, "Ve dinna need verdy much."

I brought up a few more of my trepidations, but no matter what I said, her responses were uplifting and confident. I reasoned correctly that this trait was typical of her stoic Slavic heritage. Eventually, I got a hold of myself, shut up, and ate the wonderful dinner she had prepared. Besides, during these times, pregnancy wasn't a choice.

But there was a lot to worry about. For instance, I didn't know the due date, or if it would be a boy or a girl—or even if it would be a healthy kid. And there was no way to tell. Another worry was that the baby would not be born in a hospital because there were none. There was a local doctor, but he considered childbirth too routine to warrant his services. Instead, there was a woman up in Onchiota who would come and live with you about a month before the baby was due, after which, she'd continue to stay and help out for another month. And that was all that it cost to have a baby during these times—two months of room and board for a midwife.

By far, the most considerable apprehension I had was our inadequate housing. I know that babies don't require a lot of room, at least for a few months, but they do need a healthy environment. During this time, people afflicted with a variety of ailments fled to the Adirondacks hoping its fresh air and pure water would cure them. A fair amount of these folks took rooms at the Berkeley House. I knew this because I could hear them coughing and hacking on the verandas all day and night. I also saw them wrapped in blankets and propped-up on steamship lounges in all weather. Despite the "No Invalids" sign, this hotel was still a cure cottage, but only for those who could afford it. I knew the young and the infirm are highly susceptible to contagious diseases like tuberculosis. Despite Ana's robust lineage, the act of childbirth would set her back, and I didn't want her or my kid catching their crud... But where to go?

I had a thought, and it was a long shot. But before I presented the idea to Ana, I checked with the town clerk's office. By studying old surveys and tax maps, I located the land plot of the foundation, but it showed that the land was vacant. I asked the clerk about the status of this lot and he informed me it had reverted to town ownership because of unpaid taxes. The amount of the arrears was $100.00, and since the town was eager to get the property back on the tax rolls, anyone who paid the taxes could claim the deed. I got pretty excited by this news, but I was thinking of present day finances. A hundred dollars was a little more than my annual income, plus I'd need a few bucks to make repairs to the cabin. This substantial amount of money, and the remoteness of the property, was why no one had claimed the deed.

Methodically, I worked the problem. The first step was to see if Ana could even tolerate the locality. I honestly did not know if she could tolerate living in this little shack in the woods. Some of the bravest people I know are intimidated by the solitude of the wilderness. So I motored over to Ray Brook and rummaged around the state trooper horse barns until I found the sidecar assigned to my bike. I had to scratch my head and bust a few knuckles, but I finally got the boat-like contraption attached. After this, I had to learn how to drive the Harley all over again. The steering seemed heavy, and I had a hard time not leaning around turns, but during the thrilling ride back to Saranac Lake, I got used to it.

I must admit, I wasn't looking forward to riding a motorcycle, even with a sidecar, during the freezing winter. I could not feature how a canvas tarp mounted on the handlebars would make this any better. It seemed the mechanical engineering of this time prioritized utility over comfort. Most service vehicles were open; even my boss's truck didn't have a top. I reckon they figured that it was convenient enough to ride and not have to walk.

For us lowly protectors, the commission issued us motorcycles instead of cars because they were cheaper. They were also much faster and could negotiate the rutty, obstacle-laden roads better than a car. Hell, most of the time we used these heavy "iron horses" off-road as if they were enduro-dirt bikes. Our prowess with these machines was primarily due to the commission's motor patrol trainer, Roy Holtz, who had served as a motorcycle scout during the war. Roy set up an off-road course for new riders that included jumping creeks, fording rivers, riding across logs, and climbing near-vertical hills. If you survived the course, you qualified to be issued a motorcycle instead of a horse, which was a tremendous financial benefit for a game protector.

Horses required a lot of work, not to mention you needed a place to board them. But if they issued you a horse, the commission paid a stipend for boarding. They told me that years back this allowance was more than adequate, and most enterprising game protectors would add to the windfall by selling their horse's manure to farmers for fertilizer. However, feeding and boarding expenses had increased dramatically after the war, but the compensation had remained the same. So these days, the complaint was that if you were stuck with a horse on the commission's measly stipend, there wasn't going to be any manure to sell.

On the other hand, the petrol and parts for a motorcycle were fully covered by the commission. As part of his course, Roy had trained us to perform our own maintenance, which wasn't a big reach back then because everyone was handy. So if your machine broke down, you fixed it. If you ran out of gas, you pushed it to a station and filled her up—for free. A full tank of ethylene provided about a month of patrol, except during winter. The old-time protectors, who motor-patrolled through the long North Country winters, would say, "Get her started before the first hard frost, and don't shut her off till spring!" Despite the extra fuel consumed during these nine months of idling, motorcycle patrol saved the commission a lot of money—no wonder why they encouraged them.

~*~

So my strategy was to show Ana the land and the foundation, even with the cabin in its current state of disrepair. This way if she liked what she saw, I would know she could feature living way out there. In the unlikely event she did, somehow I'd find the money to pay the taxes and fix up the cabin. *I only needed to figure out how to find money.*

It was a sunny day when I loaded Ana into the sidecar and made the twenty-mile drive. Luckily the trail was dry and we didn't get stuck. When we got there, the place looked even worse than before. It occurred to me that I had been looking at the property through rose-colored glasses because of my intimacy with it borne through watching it evolve through the eons. But with Ana alongside, I saw it through her eyes, and it wasn't a pretty sight. Or so I thought.

I didn't even dismount and was about to kick start when I heard Ana exclaim, "Dis's so beautiful! Ve could raise our family here!"

Although pleasantly shocked, I didn't trust her initial utterance. So, in disclosure (*that is semi-disclosure and not full-disclosure*), I presented a tour of buildings and grounds. First I showed her the interior of the cabin; I narrated its redacted history without revealing how I came to know it. Next, we walked to the cemetery that overlooked the vernal pond. I didn't admit that I knew those who were "resting in peace." I showed her the dilapidated paddock *where our horse and oxen once lived.* I explained the pile of rocks that once was the smokehouse. I even gave a brief tour of the leaning outhouse. Throughout the presentation, she was smiling with this dreamy look on her face. While my partial disclosure was fair and forthright, I felt a little guilty for presenting my disillusioned dream—both for Ana and the real Henry, who would have to live with the consequences. But alas, I had a reprieve, because although Ana may have been onboard, there was still no way we could pay the back taxes. Again, I was wrong.

I should have known by her homemaking proficiency Ana was a good saver. She had been dutifully saving nearly half of my (Henry's) monthly paychecks since we had married. Ana also had a significant nest egg, salted away from her teaching days. Together, we had almost $300.00 in a savings account with Adirondack Bank, plus she had squirreled away nearly as much cash that was stuffing our lumpy mattress. This made me wonder why the hell we lived like rats in that infested hotel. But as I came to realize, this was Ana's prudent nature. I paid the taxes, got the deed, and our labor of love began.

~*~

Verily, we toiled. First thing I did was fix the roof. After I removed the aberrant tree, Ana chopped it up for firewood while I braced the ridge and shingled the holes. I resisted my expedient impulse to replace the broken windows with greased paper and bought real glass from Moody's General Store in Keeseville. I had to take it easy while transporting the burlap-wrapped panes up the bumpy trail in the Harley's sidecar, which had become my new pickup truck. I had concluded that I could never remove the sidecar and had learned how to handle it well. Occasionally, I had to tell a green lie to my boss about why I had it on during the summer, but I think he knew why. Ana had done a great job of cleaning up the cabin and insisted on planting a garden while I rebuilt the paddock and smokehouse. When I questioned her timing, she advised that it wasn't too late in the season to plant potatoes and carrots.

Lucky for me was that Ana could outwork most men, even during her mid-stage of pregnancy. Although well proportioned, she was a big woman and had strength even beyond her size. I appreciated this attribute when we had to move the cast iron cook stove from the rented wagon into the cabin. That old stove was so heavy even a team of workhorses had trouble pulling it up the trail. But, with Ana's strength and my ingenuity, we got the wood-fired monstrosity into the kitchen by skidding it on greased logs. This modern convenience would take the pressure off the drafty fireplace for both tasks—heating and cooking.

As it came to be, in midsummer, we moved into the cabin. Without effort, we settled into a comfortable routine and made friends with our new surroundings. Gone was the noise of clomping horses and rattletrap automobiles of the village, and songs of the forest replaced it. Also gone was the incessant coughing and wheezing of the hotel's clients. While I felt empathy for them, I knew it was best to stay away for my family's health. Also, unlike the smoky, manure-scented village, the fragrant pine-scented air of the forest was invigorating. Even the cabin's environment was a marked improvement over the chamber-pot furnished hotel room. A short walk to the outhouse kept the cabin odor free, and our careful re-chinking of its logs kept the bugs and small critters out and the heat in. Ana was prodigious at using the two-man bucksaw and the axe. Her toil ensured we had plenty of firewood for winter. But especially gratifying for me was that Ana was happy and glowed in this new frontier. Like always, she made my homecoming each night so worthwhile. Moving our home to the foundation's cabin had given it a new lease on life and had much improved our quality of life. I only had to keep food on the table. Turns out, this wasn't so hard.

Although my job didn't pay well, it had a nice fringe benefit, and that was free protein. That's right, as long as a game protector did his job reasonably well, he could count on feeding the family with frequent seizures of fish and game seized from law violations. And, since I was good at my job, we ate well. Eventually, the commission would discontinue this benefit by instituting a policy that all evidentiary seizures of game had to be donated to charity. The intention of this new policy was to encourage the protectors to do their job properly by arresting violators *before* they killed wildlife. Regrettably, this only resulted in a lot less (official) evidence seizures and a lot more nuisance wildlife eradication—of which the protector could dispose of at his discretion. Henry was lucky because he still had two decades to work under the old policy. Who says you can't eat the bennies?

CHAPTER 14

These were the foolish things I was pondering one night as I patrolled down a dead-end woods road. Something interrupted my thoughts when I caught a whiff of burning sugar. I checked the Harley and found that nothing was awry, so I looked for other sources. Smoke appeared to be coming from the direction of a faint light in the woods. Instinctively, I cut the Harley's muffled engine, extinguished the lantern, and pushed it into the woods. Stealthily, I proceeded on foot toward the source. As I closed, the smell became more intense and familiar—it was the sweet, ethereal smell that, in a previous life, I had mistakenly associated with boiling maple sap. But as I had learned, it wasn't that then, and this wasn't it now. It was whiskey distilling.

I came to a substantial, newly constructed cabin, minimally illuminated by the dim amber glow of oil lamps. Something told me that this structure was not here a year ago, which was the last time Henry had patrolled this road. I also observed a Model TT panel truck backed in close to a side entrance. I surveilled from the tree line for about an hour, and eventually I saw the lights extinguish, one by one. Two men emerged up from this door and began loading crates into the truck. I now realized this door accessed the cabin's cellar, and despite their straw stuffing, I could tell the wooden containers contained glass by the soft clinking sound they made when jostled. The men worked up a sweat, climbing stairs and loading crate after crate, until TT's rear leaf springs were sufficiently flattened. When this predetermined limit had been reached, they started the truck, and driving without lights, they cautiously poked their way along the rutty dirt road.

This was it. Treasury Agent Baines was not just full of himself —he was full of shit! The whiskey wasn't coming from Canada, it was being made right here. All those long, boring Lake Champlain surveillances and stopping southbound vehicles with no results—it all made sense now. These entrepreneurs were maximizing profit by avoiding detection and saving shipping costs. Not to mention they were providing local jobs. But it was still illegal. I was in a quandary of what to do. Again, I had the burden of knowing prohibition didn't work, but I was sworn to uphold the law. Therefore, I had no choice. I pulled the deputy star out of my shirt pocket and pinned it to the flap.

The winds were calm and the partial moonlight revealed that both steam and smoke were coming from the chimney, so the still was still going. I figured that the two men had taken a load of booze to one of the many Lake Placid "speakeasies" and had left someone to tend the still. It was likely that they would be back soon, but probably not for at least an hour. So now was the best time to arrest the lone still operator. During these days, game protectors had no reservations about entering a dwelling without a warrant, a provision that is still allowed as long as the officer believes that the dwelling has illegal game within it. I smelled out-of-season venison roasting on that fire, so I was covered.

The last time I met with my boss, he issued me one of those new Eveready Vulcanite torches (we now call them "flashlights"). So I backtracked to the Harley and grabbed it from the sidecar, but left the Winchester in its scabbard because I figured that I would need to have my hands free so I could grapple with the still operator, who was probably drunk. Moving like a cat, I side-stepped my way to the side entrance and found the door unlocked. I drew the big Colt before going down the stairs. I could see okay with the moonlight, so I kept the torch off but kept my finger on the slide and "flash" button just in case

I needed to blind the guy. Once my boots were on the floor, I could see even better from the flickering of the freshly kindled fire burning under the base of a huge copper vessel, but I saw no one tending it. I sensed that I was alone in one big open room and that the dirt floor of the cellar was the only floor of the cabin. They had built the above grade log structure just to contain the voluminous distilling apparatus. This made it easy to confirm that I was alone, but I still needed to check things out and didn't want to ruin my night vision with the bright light of the Vulcanite, so I lit an oil lantern to have a better look around.

This was one big-ass still! The centrally located copper boiling vessel rose several feet over my head, and the condensing coils of copper rose higher yet. Suspended over the entire apparatus was a huge funnel that was the cabin's chimney, for both the smoke of fire and steam from the still. Above my head were several windows covered with burlap and a fake front door. I realized they had installed these apertures to make the cabin appear habitable. Lining the cellar's back wall were several large vats with canoe paddles sticking out. From their puke smell, I guessed that they contained mash in various stages of fermentation. I saw hundreds of glass bottles, dozens of wooden crates, and huge piles of straw against the wall near the stairs. This wasn't a backwoods moonshine distillery, this was a whiskey-making factory!

At the termination of the condensing coil, there was an automobile radiator where a barrel was positioned under its outlet. I noticed that the barrel was supported by a short platform with its spigot at just the right height to fill the bottles. I guessed that from the brief time it took someone to fill a container from this barrel was as much "barrel aging" as this whiskey would have. Yet another thing bothered me; I didn't see any separation containers for "first shots" or "tails." I didn't know a lot about distilling, but I did know the first components to boil-off the mash were mostly methanol and acetone. Reputable distillers collected this and labeled it "first shot" and used it for starting fires or cleaning drains. The "tails" were the last product to drip from the condenser because they had the highest boiling point. While not as toxic as "first shots," they consisted of headache-making fusel oils and just killed you slower. They should have separated this toxin—but they didn't!

Because of unscrupulous distillers, like these yahoos, most prospective buyers of moonshine would give it "the spoon test." That is, they would light a spoonful of the product and check the flame color. If it was red, it meant lead, which was likely the result of the distiller using a brass automobile radiator for the condenser. The lead in the brass would leach into the solvent-like condensate, and consequently contaminate the entire batch. But if the flame was yellow, it was the methanol/acetone first shot. You didn't buy either of these and only bought "blue flame" moonshine. Not surprisingly, "Blue Flame" was a popular name on bottles of backwoods booze that actually had labels. But these knuckleheads weren't separating anything— they were maximizing output by leaving the toxins in. If someone cared to give this effluent the spoon test, they would get a rainbow of color! But I was fairly sure nobody would, for it was likely that they were selling to speakeasies that were in cahoots with them. They were peddling poison—my resolve strengthened.

I shouldn't have been surprised that these dim-wits were also breaking the first rule of 'shining: "never leave a working still unattended." But they had. They must have started this batch just before they left because the kettle was just reaching a rolling boil and I heard drips of product hitting the bottom of the barrel. The harsh, toxic smell of this effluent was as overpowering as the vomit in the vats. I had to get out of here before I passed out.

I decided that it would be safest to arrest these mutts before they went inside. So I doubled back to the Harley and retrieved my rifle and staked out the distillery from across the road.

The temperature was dropping into the forties, and quite a

while had passed and yet there was no sign of them. I was getting mighty bored, along with cold and stiff from lying on the damp, moss-covered ground. *Where the hell were they?* That batch must be near done by now. *Maybe they broke down?* I risked checking my pocket watch and closed one eye, but when I pushed the flash button on the Vulcanite, nothing happened. Shit—the batteries were dead because the sliding switch was stuck in the "on" position. This had likely occurred earlier in the day, when I attempted to ride up the Whiteface Mountain trail. I had wanted to patrol this path before construction of the new Veteran's Memorial Highway began. New York's far-sighted governor, Franklin Roosevelt, had decreed that disabled veterans should be able to climb a mountain too, so for our state's first "ADA" project he was building a highway over this rugged mountain trail. But I didn't get very far along this future sightseer's road to the top because it was too rough for the sidecar. The excessive jiggling must have joggled the torch's unprotected slide switch to the "on" position, and dead batteries were my penalty for this frivolous expedition. But, lucky for me, the commission had expected these mishaps and saw fit to issue an extra set of "Cat-O-Nine Life" batteries, which were in the sidecar's glove compartment. I got up, stretched, and hobbled over to the Harley's hideout, grateful for the activity, but as I was fiddling with the torch's endcap, I heard the rattletrap truck coming down the road—and it was moving fast. I hit the dirt just in time to avoid being lit up.

Their truck was lopsided, and I realized that it must have a broken spring, which was probably why these dopes were late. I had to move quickly to get to them before they got inside, so instead of sneaking my way through the woods, I ran toward them on the road with Winchester in one hand, Vulcanite in the other. But alas, I was too slow. These guys knew they were behind schedule and were in a bigger hurry than me, for they were in the cabin door before their truck even stopped rolling. I slowed to a trot as I contemplated this new scenario. I knew it would be a lot harder to arrest them in that cavernous cabin where they had weapons and cover. I had to devise a way to draw them out.

But before I could figure this out, the cabin door flew open, and both guys flew out of it.

They were sprinting right to me, so I lit them up and shouted —"United States Treasury Agent, HALT!" But this had no effect; they were undeterred by my authority, or even by my unexpected presence. In fact, I heard one of them gasp, "Watch out, she's a gonna blow!" *Was he warning me?* Before I could take heed, the bright orange flash of an enormous fireball blinded me. An instant later, I was blown off my feet by the invisible punch of the blast wave. My last conscious thought was, *The still must have sprung a leak.*

I awoke, flat on my back, with an incredible feeling of euphoria, which only lasted until I noticed the tremendous pain I was in. My mustache and hair were singed, and my body felt like someone had beaten me with a sledgehammer, but as I unsteadily ambled to my feet, I didn't sense that anything was broken. My Stetson was long gone, but I found my rifle and flashlight. Cautiously, I negotiated through the burning debris to where I had last seen the two men. They were both face-down in the dirt, dazed and confused but otherwise in about the same shape as me. I kicked some dirt on a small fire that was still smoldering on the bigger guy's back, but before either came to, I manacled them together—left wrist of one guy to the other's right. The blast wave was significant enough to cause an implosion that sucked most of the flammable material back into the cellar, so I believed the risk of a forest fire was minimal. Satisfied, I tried to think of a way to get these guys to the judge, but their truck was crushed by a pile of logs that had landed on it. So with no good way to transport my two prisoners, I dragged them to a good sized ash tree and manacled their other wrists around it. As they gained consciousness, they bitched, complained, and even begged me not to leave them chained to the tree. But I unsympathetically advised that the smoldering fire should keep the wolves and bears away—at least for a while.

I motored the short distance to Franklin Falls, to where I knew the Paul Smith's hydro-electric plant was located. I pounded on the octagonal structure's door until I awoke the night watchman, who at first was fairly perturbed at me. But when I identified myself, drew the Colt, and said I needed to use a telephone, he became very accommodating. Again, the Essex operator graciously connected me to North Elba six, and subsequently, to my very pissed-off boss.

After I had given my location and situation report, all that he said before he hung up was, "Pull 'n' someone else's chestnuts outta the fire is only gonna git you burned fingers!"

Disheartened, I rode back to the scene, guarded my prisoners, and awaited his arrival.

It was near dawn before I heard vehicles bumping down the dirt road. One I recognized as my boss's open truck, but the other was a sleek Chevrolet utility coupe. Apparently, my boss had contacted Agent Baines who had showed up to take charge. I was glad but also annoyed that Agent Baines was not the least bit conciliatory about putting us on a wild goose chase. Instead, in his folksy way, he acted like he had known the booze was being made locally all along. I couldn't tell if it was an act or he was just full of more shit.

When my boss questioned him on this, Baines said, "Why the hell else would I call on you game cops to find these clandestine stills—you boys know these Godforsaken woods."

Agent Baines further explained that the Treasury Department had been surveilling this New York City organized crime mob that imported this poison from Lake Placid but couldn't find the source. He also stated that he had long suspected that the poisoned whiskey was being made in the States, but his bosses in the White House found it politically expedient to blame Canada—presumably so they could provide funding for the new Border Patrol Agency. But Baines realized that it would be years before this agency would become effective, so he convinced his immediate supervisor to allow him to deputize wildlife officers in the Northeast to help with the deadly booze epidemic that was plaguing New York City.

He further explained that's why he had to give us the company line about shipments coming from up north, but he said, "I knew you boys would go about your squirrel sheriff bidness, but you'd also be work'n' fer me."

He also informed that he had deputized fish and game officers in Maine and Vermont, and the Vermont Game Wardens had found a similar operation—a fake log cabin in the middle of nowhere with a big-ass, two-story still.

He added that these two mopes I had arrested were small fish, and they usually kept their mouths shut and did their jail time. "But since these incompetents had blown up one of their employer's major distilleries, even these boneheads would know their life in prison would be shortened by a shanking."

"Consequently," Agent Baines said, "these here boys will sing like a couple of canaries."

He further added that they would likely reveal the location of other distilleries, methods of covert transportation, and even the names of higher ups. With this info, the Treasury Department could conduct a sweep from Lake Placid to the City and shut the operation down for good.

All of this seemed to put my boss in an even lousier mood, probably because he was thinking about the price of his favorite beverage going up.

Sensing his darkening mood, Agent Baines offered, "Because of you boy's heroic efforts on this case, I might be able to get a few of them new army general purpose vehicles assigned to you fish cops fer testing."

These GP scout vehicles that the army had spec'd were the forerunners of the infamous four-wheel-drive "Jeeps." They would be perfect for patrol and a lot warmer than a motorcycle during winter.

At this, my boss clapped my sore back and said, "Good job, Henry!"

CHAPTER 15

I was never this happy in my life—*past or present ones,* but there were a few things that gave me pause. One was that when I first saw the foundation, it was in a state of declination, with no evidence of a cabin structure. I couldn't fathom how all those logs could decompose in… what…ninety-five years? At first, I attributed this mystery to a forest fire, but I recalled during my first viewing, I saw huge trees that were living, or had matured and died within the foundation. They should be saplings growing from the cellar floor right now—but they weren't!

Also, I believed my fiddling with the stone shelf somehow violated the temporal paradox which was my return ticket to the present. Specifically, moving the stone violated "The Grandfather Paradox," which states that a time traveler can do anything that *did happen,* but can't do anything that *didn't happen.* I reasoned that was why I got booted back to the present whenever I tried to move it—the stone was a permanent part of the foundation and I wasn't allowed to change that. *But hadn't I already violated this paradox many times, in many other ways?* I had been here for over five months—far longer than any previous time trip—*and during this time I had changed many things, notwithstanding restoring the cabin.* It didn't add up.

Also, thinking of the time, I wondered what was happening to my present self *while I was frolicking in this life.* Had I frozen to death? I remember being chilled to the bone before unexpectedly "going back." Or…were coywolves gnawing on my carcass as I was enjoying this retro-life in paradise? I took solace because my previous experiences of "going back" had amounted to mere minutes of real time, *but even so, half of a year in dream time must equate to a significant amount of real time?*

Most of me wanted to stay. I had it pretty damn good during this episode, especially when compared to my previous time trips, where I was unfamiliar with the times and at an evolutionary disadvantage. I could not help comparing this retro-life in the past to my present real-life situation. While here, I was a revered game protector, unlike my present life status as a pensioner and part-time handyman. Also, in this life, I was young again, had a loving wife, and was soon to be a father. But back in the present, I had a cheating wife and was a senior citizen with a warrant on my head. While here, I was living the dream. But that was it—deep inside, *I knew it was a dream. What to do, what should I do?*

Unlike my last temporal experience, I had bonded with my environment—the cabin, my occupation, the period, and especially my comfy home life. But like the last time, I realized that my reluctance to leave was because I had bonded with my avatar and with Ana. *What would become of them when, and if, I go? Would Henry continue to be the innovative provider and loving husband? What would become of Ana—and what about the baby?* Thoughts like this were going to make my head explode.

I further understood that if I stayed, assuming I could stay here, that I'd have to go through The Great Depression and the next World War—but I'd have the advantage of having watched all those History Channel episodes, so I'd know how to manage. So much for the Grandfather paradox!

Having thought of this, I also recognized, if I returned, this would likely be my last trip *or at least my last trip "back" in time.* My reasoning was that each progression of "going back" seemed to get later in time and closer to the present, and there wasn't enough time left before I would be born *again* in 1956. If I dropped in at...let's say 1960, I might experience the awkward event of meeting my four-year-old self. I didn't think the paradoxes of time travel or the Great Spirits would allow this. I wouldn't want to see myself, either—way too weird. If I went back, it would be a one-way trip.

But maybe returning to deal with my issues wasn't a bad thing. I had learned much through these experiences, and I could put these lessons to use for the good of all mankind. Well, actually, that was a stretch. What I really meant was that I could write a book from my prison cell. That's right, even though *in this life* I was busier than a one-legged man in an ass-kicking contest, the thought of the misdeeds of my present life were never far from my consciousness. I had read once "that peace of mind was the highest order of existence"—and I didn't have it. I needed to resolve this.

There was that, and there was one more rumble of thunder in the distance I had *deliberately* been ignoring—I missed Marlene! Even though *in my mind* she was a cheating, spoiled, highfalutin' bitch, I was still attracted to her. Moreover, I missed her passion and the hunger of her arousal. I didn't have that here. Through this adventure, I came to love Ana, but only with affection and not with passion—as if she were a sibling. Testament to this was that Henry's testosterone-raging, thirty-year-old form hadn't had sex with her since the baby's conception. Even more disparaging was that Ana seemed to be good with this.

At some point during this latest episode, my anger had disappeared and it was replaced with guilt. Throughout my time with Ana, I felt like the model husband—a heroic and compassionate provider. *Why hadn't I been like this with Marlene, or had I been? Was it her strong character that intimidated me into feeling less? Was I still holding her hostage to her pedigree?* Shame on me!

I still had this longing for Marlene, and in my disillusioned mind, I decided that we could patch things up and rekindle the fire. History is filled with men who have sacrificed much for love and sex. Here I was, willing to shorten my lifespan by more than thirty years and give up a dream life just to get laid. *It's weird, how thot works.*

As I went through the permutations of outcomes, I had to keep in mind I had hurt no one—*I had just damaged a car, albeit an expensive car.* So it was likely that I wouldn't be writing this book from prison. Instead, I'd be doing community service, and the court would garnish my paltry pension to buy Fast Freddie a new Beemer. This would require that I get serious about earning another income, but I could do that, for I'd gotten damn good at roofing, shoveling, and all manner of handyman tasks. Also, off-season, camp caretakers were always in demand; I only had to find one of those gigs that wouldn't require risking my life by shoveling a three-story roof. *Or...maybe I could work as a game warden for one of those private hunting clubs?*

Without regard to what would become of me, I couldn't shake the feeling that in this life, I was an imposter, living a lie. Sometimes I felt as though Ana knew this, but more often I thought the character that played my boss had me nabbed. During our few interactions, he would morph from the grumpy, hard drinking game cop to the kindly, all-knowing, Adirondack guide, and back again. *Hadn't I seen him in the last life as a town clerk and in my present life at the Grille?* Why did he keep coming back—*was he guiding me toward something?*

Thus, these were the thoughts swimming in the murky waters of my noggin when I decided that I would go home. Like the last time I left, I wanted to leave everything in order, sort of like cleaning your house before you go away *just in case you don't come back.* I washed the Harley, cleaned my guns, polished all duty leather, and brought in a load of wood for the stove. Ana, hardy as ever, barely showed any effects of her pregnancy, but even so, I didn't want her lugging unnecessarily heavy loads. I had to keep reminding myself *you'll leave, but Henry remains, he'll take care of her, he loves her too.*

Being mindful of her routine, I waited for Ana to leave for her firewood-gathering walk. I knew this would last about two hours, which was plenty of time for Henry to reorient himself without me. *If that was even necessary?* Overwhelmed with nostalgia, I marveled *for the last time* at some repairs I had made to the fireplace. I snatched a candle off of its new mantle and headed down into the cellar. Lighting the candle wasn't necessary because it was a bright sunny day, and consequently there was plenty of light coming through the gaps in the floor planking overhead. But I lit it anyway for ambiance and because I wanted to see and remember every detail of the foundation like this—in its heyday. I walked to the shelf and carefully placed the lit candle on my gateway to home. I set my stance and gripped firmly on each side of the thick, cold slab. I took one last look around and pulled. But it didn't move, so I pushed, with the same result—so I pushed even harder. In a panic, I tried lifting and pressing down—nothing! It was as if welded. The candle upon it didn't even flicker! Sweating, I shielded the candle with my hand and looked beyond the flame and into the foundation strata that supported the cantilevered shelf. What I saw made me gasp for breath, for the years of frost had shifted the massive support stones, permanently wedging the shelf in place.

I also noticed the sharp grayish-blue features of the stones had faded to a shadowy reddish-brown. I had lost my color vision. At this realization, a peculiar feeling befell me, and it wasn't one that I had experienced before—it was one of ethereal timelessness. My heart raced, I felt weightless, and I was fading away—*but not "going to" anywhere.* Fearful and with the last of my consciousness, I tugged, trying to shake the stone laterally from side to side. It was useless—I was stuck.

With fading awareness, I heard the cabin door fly open, and the frantic voices of both Ana and my boss. By the dust falling through the cracks in the floor, I sensed that they were directly overhead, and they were desperately calling me—*but...they were calling me...Mason!?*

CHAPTER 16

Her phone was ringing. *But who was calling so early?* As soon as the thought passed, Marlene realized that she knew who was calling and why. The ringing finally stopped—*but were they leaving a message.*

By the brightening eastern horizon, she estimated it to be about 5 a.m. Her feet hit the icy floor. She should rekindle the fire and make some coffee before checking for messages.

But maybe it was Fred who had called? As her best friend, he often called at odd hours, in turmoil regarding his tempestuous love life. She had slipped once and advised him that his lifestyle wasn't the best choice in these parts. The next time they'd spoken, he had kindly informed her that being gay wasn't a choice. Of course she knew that. She'd merely meant that there were slim pickings for dating for anyone in the North Country. But there was no need to kick that horse again. Their friendship had prevailed over many of Fred's hypersensitive hissy-fits.

There were still some glowing coals in the fire, so she only needed to add a few pine cones and kindling to get it blazing again. She loaded a few more splits and then some big round logs for endurance. Marlene was so glad that she had convinced Mason to install wood heat over propane. While propane would have been convenient, wood was free. And heating with wood warmed you twice if you split it yourself, as she did.

After a second cup of coffee, it was time. She removed her iPhone from the signal-boosting dock and called voicemail.

The call was from Dr. Abideo: "Marlene, call me. There was

a change last night, and we need to discuss our options." She already knew what those options were: *life or death.* And...the good doctor wanted her to pull the plug. Bitterly, she wept.

Mason's response to the accident was still perplexing. Luckily, Uncle Ted had been watching his webcam when Mason had tumbled off Camp Thaddy's roof. He had called right away. She had reached out to one of Mason's forest ranger buddies, Captain Stripe, who immediately organized a rescue. The rangers used their new AirBoat to transport Mason, still unconscious, across the thin ice to Saranac General. He was hypothermic and frostbitten, but thanks to falling into the deep pile of snow, his brain was uninjured—which was why Dr. Abideo couldn't explain his prolonged coma.

It had been six weeks now, and Mason showed only minimal brain activity. Over the past month, his condition had worsened. On occasion, he had even stopped breathing. Dr. Abideo had been quick to remind Marlene of Mason's health care proxy, which clearly stated that he didn't want any heroic measures to maintain his life. But here he was, intubated, with intravenous feeding and waste collection bags hanging under his hospital bed—he would be furious that she had allowed this. But that's what love does—it causes you to hang on to memories and hope.

Come back Mason, please—just come back.

As Marlene turned the key of her ten-year-old Jeep Cherokee, she realized that it sounded like its age, with a lot of whining and groaning as it caught and shook to life—but, at least it always started. While she knew the Jeep wasn't the best vehicle to impress her clientele, it was capable and had often pulled Fred's very impressive BMW out of an unplowed client's driveway.

They were a codependent team and perhaps this was one reason they worked so well together. Depending on the situation, Fred would pick up the prospects at the Adirondack Regional Airport and show the property. With his native Australian accent and superb descriptive creativity, he could paint scenes of the future owners sitting by a roaring fire with cocktails after a thrilling day of skiing Whiteface. When Fred thought he had sufficiently set the hook deep enough, he'd just happen to stop by their Lake Placid office, where Marlene would be waiting to reel them in. This tag-team technique had worked well in the past, but now it seemed the only people looking to buy property in the North Country were either the very wealthy or the very capable.

The wealthy ones would fly in private jets and have their consorts at Berkshire-Hathaway, or some other non-local-yokel firm, show the estate. Often, these clueless, urbane Realtors would contact Marlene's company for a preview of the address they were selling. When she offered to do this for a percentage of their commission, the calls stopped. Word traveled quickly within the Realtor community.

But, as Marlene often explained to Fred, without regard to who got the commission, the wealthy buyers were good for the North Country economy in other ways. For example, local contractors could count on a faux-rustic remodel of their new camp, and maybe the same for the boathouse. They also hired locals for the silliest things, like cutting firewood, cleaning chimneys, and even house cleaning. Additionally, some lucky local would get the contract for caretaking of the property for the fifty weeks of the year when it wasn't being used. "Cottage Caretaking" was a burgeoning cottage industry in the North Country because no one had the time to take care of their camps these days. Added to the economic bonus was that the real estate commissions on these high-end properties recurred about every five years. While the mechanism behind this phenomenon was interesting, it wasn't very complicated.

Understandably, these overstressed rich folks wanted a place in the woods to "get away from it all," but they also wanted to bring civilization into the wilderness with them. Their first shock occurred when their smartphones didn't work and continued to compound when they realized that only slow-speed internet was available—typically via a satellite dish. The ECOs and rangers would have a field day writing tickets to them for hauling their butterball asses into the designated Wilderness Areas on their brand-new All-Terrain Vehicles, an area where motor vehicles were expressly prohibited. Adding to this insult was when they tried to have street lights and swimming pools installed, or when they cleared the forest for a private golf course; the Adirondack Park Agency would issue an injunction. This order would stop the assault, require habitat reconstruction, and usually levy a substantial fine. Occasionally, the novice camp owners would have their team of city lawyers fight the injunction—at great expense, and with negative results. When combined, these noisome nuisances would frequently make the property available on the market again. *The black flies aren't the only "saviors of the Adirondacks!"*

The capable prospects, although much more pleasant to deal with than the wealthy ones, frequently only wanted to buy land, where the commissions were fairly trivial. For showing land to these potential buyers, Marlene's Jeep was just fine, and often appreciated because of its practical nature. These people would go about building their "cabin in the woods" and actually live there all year round. They cut their own wood, cleaned their own house (and usually several others), and fixed everything themselves. Other than paying taxes and buying groceries, they contributed little to the North Country economy. Even so, they were the best neighbors.

Marlene took a last look at the cabin before negotiating her long driveway, which was essentially a road through the woods. As a not so well thought out strategy, she had Hadden's Garage install a plow on Mason's old truck. Marlene had quickly learned how to use it and could clear the entire mile of road in about thirty minutes, but that was only when the truck started. Unlike her Jeep, the old Dodge often wouldn't cooperate, and she'd have to call Mason's former employer, Rudeau's, to plow her out.

In hindsight, she realized that they were a better value than the new plow.

But the light dusting of last night's snow didn't require that Marlene try starting the truck this morning. As she caught one last glimpse in the rearview mirror, Marlene thought the fresh snow made the homestead appear even more picturesque. Although she loved it, she knew her lifestyle didn't meld with her profession of selling luxury vacation properties. According to her prospective clients, Marlene was camping—full time.

This disparity of her profession and housing choice was also true of their first house, a short-sale that Marlene had found in her Realtor newsletter. To the uninformed, this property didn't seem to be very "Adirondacky" at all. In fact, it looked more like a typical ranch-style house, albeit a long one. But it was actually an Adirondack historical treasure, being a former lumberjack camp that was built in the 1800s. A lot of folks didn't realize that, aside from tiny seasonal trapper cabins, the original Adirondackers didn't build sprawling log cabins, at least not after someone had invented the sawmill. The lumberjack camp's construction of rough-sawn timbers and planks was a testament to that. Its simple open floor plan, consisting of a kitchen at one end and a massive stone fireplace at the other, was elegant. Mason had installed a beautiful bathroom, complete with a jetted tub, but against her protests, he tore down the two-stall outhouse in the backyard. Marlene thought it would have made a great toolshed for her gardening hobby, but Mason said it stunk and was an eyesore. The one thing she held firm on was that he could not remove the rusty iron padeye rings that lined the home's interior walls. Mason said they were for hanging wet clothing and were now useless, but Marlene countered that they represented the heritage of the house. To validate their usefulness, she hung Mason's wet hunting outfit from a line strung across the two nearest the woodstove. He never talked of removing them again. Like most disputes, she won whenever she wanted to.

Marlene still owned the property, but because of its non-rustic architecture, and since it wasn't on the waterfront, the old lumberjack camp wasn't worth much as a vacation rental. Actually, the insurance quotes were more than she would net from the short ski season, which seemed to get shorter every year. Added to this were the costs of renovations, as the wood-stove would need removal, the fireplace blocked, and electric heat installed to make the rental idiot-proof. Even if Mason did the work, she would still have a significant business loss for tax time—*yet another one she didn't need.*

But the property was worth keeping for its detached garage that Mason used for his hobby business as a contractor. So the substantial, and convenient, lumberjack bunkhouse remained vacant while they lived in a tiny cabin in the interior wilderness, which was so remote, even the locals described it as being "way out there."

But Marlene would counter that they had everything she needed. Although they were off the grid, Mason had ingeniously provided them with electricity via solar and wind generation. The cabin's running water was pressurized by gravity, piped from a spring box up the hill. Hot water was provided by the wood-fired boiler in the cellar, which also efficiently heated the modest cabin.

Near as anyone could tell, someone built the native log cabin in the 1800s and someone else remodeled it during the 1920s. It was what the Realtors labeled as "open architecture," meaning it was one big room. But at least it had a cozy sleeping loft, and thankfully, Mason had installed an indoor bathroom—complete with a composting toilet. Marlene also loved the river-rock fireplace that occupied the cabin's entire north wall, which she occasionally used for its ambiance. But oddly, the feature she liked the most about the cabin was its cellar.

It was a real stone foundation. Huge stacked boulders formed plumb walls, and overhead, roughhewn timber joists supported the solid plank floor. The planks had shrunk over the years, leaving substantial gaps, which allowed light from above, and heat from the boiler to rise. This kept the cabin toasty in even the coldest weather and provided enough light for most tasks. But if Marlene needed more light, she had only to light the candle sitting on the stone slab shelf, permanently set in the foundation's corner. With light from above and heat from below, it was a simple but elegant design.

Marlene also loved the wilderness setting. A few miles to the east there was a beautiful riverine valley, where Mason idled away many a fall day, presumably hunting deer. Just up-hill from the cabin was a vernal pond where a cemetery with five unmarked crosses stood. Mason meticulously maintained them as if he knew those buried beneath each one. But he was funny about this. Mason denied knowing the residents of the cemetery, and when asked why he spent so much time there, he would sidestep by saying, "I'm only showing respect to those who were here first." Marlene suspected that there was more to this saga.

Mason said he had inherited the land and cabin from his grandparents, Henry and Ana Hawkins. They had an only child which was presumably Mason's father, but Mason only spoke of his grandparents, as though his parents didn't exist. The other perplexing thing was that Mason's surname was his grand-mother's maiden name, Brocke, which the officials changed from Bjrozc at Ellis Island when the family emigrated from Serbia. Mason also claimed his grandmother raised him, since his grandfather, being some kind of lawman, was killed in a gunfight with bootleggers. *But where were his mom and dad?* Mason was tight-lipped about his family history, and what little Marlene had learned she got during interrogations when he was half asleep and fully drunk. She was sure that there was a dark family secret that he didn't want her to know. *But what could that be—was Mason a love child? Did his parents split-up and aban-don him? Could that be why Ana Brocke had raised him?* Weirder than weird! A true North Country mystery.

Among the many things she loved about the homestead was the wintertime scenery. The leafless trees afforded great views of the High Peaks that the summer foliage blocked. More than once she had to remind Mason not to be overzealous with his chainsaw, lest they get hit with a view tax. The threat of this dreaded tax would keep his saw quiet for about a month. Tears blurred her vision as she thought of Mason not being around to use his saw, or any of his tools, again.

The wispy cirrus clouds in the clear blue sky indicated to Marlene that more snow was coming, but probably not until later in the week. It really didn't matter, for she could have driven to the hospital in a blizzard. In fact, she had, several times, as she had been visiting Mason every day for the past six weeks. But if Dr. Abideo was correct, this might be her last time, the thought of which brought another wave of despair. Why did Mason make his proxy irrevocable? In an instant the answer came to her—he was a biologist, and he understood too well the consequences of living in a state of morbidity.

Dr. Abideo was an enigma, or at least he was to Marlene. She described his appearance as "scruffy," and for all the world, he looked like he was more at home on a log skidder than in an operating room. But he was a gifted physician and the go-to guy for any procedure from cardiac bypasses for the elderly to orthopedic surgery on Olympic athletes. And despite his Mediterranean-sounding name, he was, as he described himself, a purebred Adirondican. In fact, Marlene thought he went out of his way to look this part with his untrimmed, white hair and beard. Moreover, he often did his bedside rounds, sans white coat, swaggeringly displaying his checkered flannel shirt and suspendered Malone pants. Marlene thought he looked as if he were in costume as an old-time guide.

They had moved Mason into a private room for his final hours. That's all that a Cadillac health insurance plan affords you these days, thought Marlene. In accord with the executed proxy, they had discontinued the intubation. Marlene also noticed that the incessantly beeping monitors were gone, likely for her benefit. But Mason was still breathing. Dr. Abideo said this may continue for several hours or even for several days until Mason's autonomic nervous system decided that it was time; and then, according to the good doctor, he would just peacefully go to sleep—no drugs needed.

But again, Mason's color was excellent, and throughout this ordeal, he hadn't lost weight or muscle. It was as if his synapses were firing, unnoticed, and causing isometric muscle contractions—keeping him fit and toned. In fact, without all the tubes and monitors, he looked as healthy as ever, like he was just napping and would wake-up at any moment. Marlene thought it didn't matter that he would never awaken; she would continue to read to him as she had every day since the accident.

Mason loved Adirondack history, a penchant he developed from one of his college professors, a biology prof named Dr. Torrance, as she recalled. So before heading to her office, Marlene dutifully read to him every day, for at least an hour. When she finished reading *The Adirondack Reader* by Jamison, Marlene continued with the classic *Adirondack Country* by William Chapman White. And after those, Marlene read *A Game Warden's Diary* by Chauncey Weitz. But lately, she had been reading about the Prohibition Era, from archives of the *Adirondack Almanack*. While she thought those articles were interesting, they had also taught her more about making moonshine than she ever cared to know.

At the inception of this tragedy, Marlene was wholly unprepared for Mason's long internment at Saranac General. When Dr. Abideo suggested that reading to Mason might help him recover, all she had with her were unexciting real estate listings on her phone. With scant choice, Mason's daily readings began with a dusty book she found in the waiting room, called *The Foundation* by a guy named Dean. It was a weird-ass story about geo-time travel or some nonsense, and she was glad to be done with it. But, despite suffering through it and the *Almanacks*,

Marlene sincerely hoped that on some level Mason enjoyed the readings. For her, it was a labor of love and she was grateful to have had the time with him.

Dr. Abideo had graciously stopped by while doing his rounds. She noticed that he was wearing his Mackinaw coat and felt crusher hat, likely about to leave the hospital for a hike or whatever he did during his lunch. Presently, Mason was breathing deeply, his chest rising and falling rapidly, just as if he was working out. This action apparently piqued Dr. Abideo's interest because he removed his coat and listened to Mason's vitals with his stethoscope.

Concerned, Marlene asked, "What's going on, Doc?"

To which he replied, "I'm not sure—but I don't think he's quite ready to leave us."

At this declaration, Marlene called Mason's name, as did Dr. Abideo. To their amazement, Mason responded by thrusting his arms out, as if he were reaching for something, something big. Other than a few reflexive tremors, this was the first time he had moved in weeks. It was a miracle. Dr. Abideo abruptly called for assistance and a crash cart, as he continued to assess Mason's vitals.

Mason's arms were flailing wildly now, as if he were pushing and pulling, his muscles taut and straining against some immovable object. Then suddenly, as quickly as it began, it was over. Mason's arms relaxed, dropped to his side, and his body went slack.

But, he was breathing, and his eyes were open!

Mason smiled as he looked at Marlene.

EPILOGUE

It's just after sunrise, and I'm sitting with a cup of coffee on the cabin's new deck I finished last week. The mourning doves are cooing, and the turkeys are a'gobbling. The woodpeckers are sending code via the Adirondack telegraph by pecking on the birdhouse I built last month. I reckon that its hollowness makes for a good pecker amplifier? Despite the racket, it's a beautiful spring morning—a morning full of brilliant color.

It has been over a year since I've had my little flying lesson off of Uncle Ted's camp roof, and I'm pretty much patched up. Marlene says that I was laid up for six weeks, four days, and five hours. But despite being unconscious for most of that time, I'm better than before. For one thing, I seem to have more time to do domestic things, and I think Marlene appreciates that almost as much as I do. Also, I've got to remark that it was generous of Uncle Ted to pick up the tab for my lengthy hospital stay. My insurance would have covered most of it, but, thanks to him, Marlene didn't even have a copay.

I know that I dreamed a lot while I was out, but damned if I can remember any of them. Like most dreams, they evaporated in the light of day. But occasionally, I'll get a flash of something wonderful and terrifying at the same time. For example, I have visions of being a beast while men are chasing me through a forest. I have expectations of inanimate objects talking—like rocks and trees. Weird! Other times, I have images of wearing a uniform and doing heroic things, and of being a provider for a family. Equally weird! But none of that matters now, because I'm back, and I am ever so glad.

My summer will be busy this year because the college wants me to conduct two sessions of Adirondack Biology. My reviews of last summer's class were off the chart, with the students expressly commenting on my campfire storytelling. *I have no idea what caused this change.* Yet, this year's class is oversubscribed—by four-fold! So the college has asked me to add another session to avoid complaints. Next year, I'm going to break in another instructor to take over. A whole month of camping is too much for me, and for some reason, sleeping in a tent gives me a deep chill—even during the summer.

Besides, I need time to supervise my building construction crew. That's right; I had to hire two carpenters and a mason because I couldn't keep up with all the new business, which includes everything from boathouses to camp additions. Go figure—ever since Marlene's business partner, Fredrick, helped me set up a website, my inbox is loaded with requests for jobs. It's funny. Local Adirondackers don't think much of the internet, but the camp owners from downstate sure do. Fred is a great salesman and knows how to present. He knew exactly how to display "Brocke Builders Inc." with the right amount of rustic flare without being "over the top."

Fred charged me for registering the site and would only accept a growler of Leaning Pine IPA for his labor. Did I mention that he's a good guy and a great friend?

This fall is going to be a busy one, too, because the Powderhorn Hunting Lodge has hired me, again, as their game keeper. Last year, when I signed on, I thought I would be just managing the wildlife for the 3000-acre club. But when the board gave me an ATV with a rifle in the scabbard and also issued me a green military-style uniform, I realized that there would be a little more to this job. Thankfully, it mostly involves enforcement of trespass on the club's property. But I've made several citizen arrests for poaching. These were fairly exciting experiences with the offender's becoming belligerent and then violent. Some-how, I handled them and took them into custody, *and yet, I don't know how I knew to do this.* Perhaps I've watched too many cop shows.

With the extra dough I've been bringing in, I offered to buy Marlene that Lexus SUV that she's been pining for. To my sur-prise, she wouldn't have it. Instead, she wanted a Jeep Wrangler. When I asked why, she said it was more important to get up our road and come home to me than it was to impress her clients. So the Jeep it was because when you've got a woman that loves living in the woods, you take care of her. To be honest, her words have deeply moved me.

I think Marlene has a point, though; the time we spend to-gether at home is priceless. Living and loving in the wilderness —what could be better? When I think of our brave little cabin and how it has prevailed for over a century, I feel a tremendous sense of place. Moreover, when I think of the eons of time that its stone foundation has stood—I am awestruck.

I built this deck on the backside of the cabin so it wouldn't ruin its traditional lines. It also provides a beautiful view, es-pecially during the spring, right before the bright green leaves come out. But since they're still red buds, I can see the ver-nal pond from it, even when slouching in my Adirondack chair. And, if I look real hard, I can make out the wooden crosses of the cemetery next to it. They mark the sacred resting places of those who came before me. I'm not sure who they all are, but I feel an unexplainable familiarity with each of them.

Time and weather have rotted their original stick and log crosses, so I've replaced them with native cedar, which should last well beyond me. To the best of my ability, I've tried to de-cipher their names and carve it into each crossbar. The easiest ones were the most recent, for Ana and Henry, the previous in-habitants of our home. There were also two large log crosses and a small one made of sticks. I could only make out a first letter "J" followed by an "O" on the small one. So I reckoned that this marker was likely for a child named Joseph. One of the large log crosses seemed to have a biblical name, which I determined to be "Hezekiah." However, despite my best effort, the name on the oldest cross was rotted to the point of being illegible. I don't know why, but I assumed that it was Hez's wife, and since it was a Sunday when I replaced it, I named her "Domenica."

When I tend the cemetery, a peaceful but yet peculiar feeling befalls me—it's as if I'm sensing the eons of time that this hallowed ground has endured. I don't know what happens or where we go when we die, or if we go anyplace. But if we do, I know I won't be going to heaven, because I'm already here. I'm not one to be overly religious, but I give thanks to my God every day for this good life.

On the other hand, *what if there is an afterlife and you do go to another place?* If there is, and you do, it has got to be pretty crowded. Consequently, given where I live, I wouldn't want to go there. I've read that some religions teach that you when you die you go back and inhabit the body of one of your ancestors and relive that life to improve it, while completely forgetting about the previous life you had.

I could go for that—just not yet.

Acknowledgement:

Thank you. I do appreciate your readership.
If you enjoyed *The Foundation*, please consider leaving a review.
Again, I thank you.

Capt. Samuel Dean

ABOUT THE AUTHOR

Samuel Dean is a retired captain of the New York State
Environmental Conservation Police and a USCG licensed
captain. His hobbies include capturing the past in humorous
short stories and restoring old motorcycles that many have
said cannot be done. He resides in Lake Placid, NY.

For more about the author and his other stories, see his
author page: amazon.com/author/samueldean

Made in the USA
Middletown, DE
28 July 2019